ARMSTRONG

ARMSTRONG

ALEC WHITNEY

PUBLISHED FOR THE CRIME CLUB BY
DOUBLEDAY & COMPANY, INC.
GARDEN CITY, NEW YORK
1977

All of the characters in this book
are fictitious, and any resemblance
to actual persons, living or dead,
is purely coincidental.

ISBN: 0-385-12680-8
Library of Congress Catalog Card Number 76–42411

Printed in the United States of America

To Michele

ARMSTRONG

PROLOGUE

On his way to the police station in Beacon Gardens, Detective Inspector Armstrong saw the poster outside the Royal Hall announcing "AN EVENING WITH BEETHOVEN." The orchestra was the Paris State Symphony, its guest conductor Otto Flughafer. The time was just before half past two on the day of the concert. Armstrong smiled ruefully; that evening he would be on duty. He was so preoccupied with the poster that he didn't notice the man wearing a brown technicians' coat and carrying a long brown canvas bag with the initials BBC stamped on it walk through the artists' entrance with the orchestra and the members of the Bradford Choir who were to sing the last, choral, movement of the Ninth Symphony.

The man lifted the bag and showed its initials to the doorman. "Microphone on the blink," he said, and the doorman nodded without interest.

The BBC broadcasts so frequently from the Royal Hall that it keeps a permanent set-up of microphones, amplifiers, and a control room in a converted box, with mixers and direct lines to Broadcasting House and thence to the Television Centre.

The man in the brown coat didn't go into the BBC box. He climbed the stairs to the roof, opened a fanlight, and, with a length of wood taken from his bag, propped it open so he could look down into the Hall.

The rehearsal was about to begin.

He took three pieces of iron from his bag and bolted

them together to form a tripod. He fastened the legs of the tripod into the asphalt of the roof using a hand drill and expanding bolts. On the top of the tripod he mounted a long tube about eight inches in diameter, also taken from his bag, and pointed it into the auditorium using a telescopic sight he clipped to its side. He locked the nuts securing the tube and took off the sight. Then he tested the firmness of the tube by attempting to shake it. It did not move.

A lever about one inch long hung below the tube near its centre and when he inserted the key of a clockwork motor into the side of the tube and turned it, the lever moved forward. When it had travelled its full extent he unclipped a handle mounted in the side of the tube and pulled it back. There was a click. The man smiled, paused to listen to the orchestra which had started rehearsing below. He frowned a little and nodded his approval when Flughafer stopped them to make a correction, then turned his attention back to the tube on the tripod. From the pocket of his brown coat he took what looked like a small transistor radio. He held it three feet from the tube and switched it on. No audible sound came from it but the clockwork mechanism on the barrel of the tube started to turn, the lever moved slowly backwards, and when it reached the end of its short travel the slide above it whanged forward, metal striking metal inside the tube. The man had the half smile of a satisfied technician. He wound the clockwork, pulled back the slide, and set the mechanism again. Then he clipped a thin, curved metal box to the top of the tube above the slide. Finally he draped the assembly in a grey plastic cover on which were stencilled in blood red the words

BBC: LIVE TERMINALS: DANGER.

It was three o'clock on the afternoon of the concert. Detective Inspector Armstrong was sitting alone in the inspectors' room of the Beacon Gardens police station, only two minutes' walk from the Royal Hall. Brodsky was off sick, Carmichael had taken an overdue week of holiday, Pemberton was out on an investigation. Armstrong looked up at the wall clock and swore gently. Three o'clock. Too early to ask the canteen for a cup of tea and his throat was dry as the files he was condemned to reading. He pushed them from him in disgust and motes of dust rose into the beam of sunlight that fell on the corner of his desk, as if he'd suddenly exhaled a lungful of cigarette smoke. So much to do, so much to be done. And most of it paper work. Armstrong, in common with almost every other copper he knew, didn't like paper work. He liked to be out and about, among the crowds, actively working on an investigation. He liked talking to people, especially criminals, the cut and thrust, the challenge of knowing when they were lying, when they were telling what passed for the truth. Some coppers were physical and preferred pushing their weight about. Others were cerebral, watching and waiting, thinking and reasoning. Armstrong liked to think he was the latter type, though he could move hard when he had to. As he sat at his desk he was conscious of these things battling each other in his mind: the longing for action, but his distrust of action without thought; the need for carefully collated paper work, and his dislike of pen pushing.

"That's the trouble with a copper's life," Armstrong thought. "You never get time to think, never get a chance to work out a position in advance." Right now he ought to be thinking about the dozens of cases he was involved in; that silver job, for example, and that break-in at the clothing shop, and that business with the phoney M.O.T. test certificates, and . . . oh, the list was endless. You never had time to sit down and take them all apart, unravel the tangled skeins of thought that cluttered your mind like a drawer full of mixed mending wools. A copper had a personal life too, didn't he, and that often got mixed in with the rest. Right now, for instance, he'd like to be enjoying his private life. He'd like to be at that Beethoven concert, just listening to the music. How typical that he should like classical music when the rest of his colleagues would rather go to the Palladium than the Royal Hall; just another of the many barriers between him and the rest of them, the many differences that made him sometimes suspect, an odd man out. There were so many things he'd like to be doing, not all of them self-indulgent. He'd like to make a page of notes about that M.O.T. test certificate job; the answer to that job was there, somewhere, probably staring him in the face if only he could take a half an hour off and just *think* about it. He'd half a mind to do just that when he saw the note again, the one he'd stuck in the corner of his blotter. EXPENSE ACCOUNTS, the note said, and was underlined in red. Bloody paper work.

He drew forward a stack of papers an inch high, D/1 and D/5 expenses vouchers he had to approve, initial, and pass upstairs. He looked at the first one with real loathing. A D/5 for Sergeant Boskin. He liked Sergeant Boskin, knew him to be a good conscientious sergeant, but staring at that form he almost hated the man for causing paper work. He began reading the form. Then he sighed, picked up the telephone, and dialled an internal extension. Boskin himself answered from the detectives' room.

"Your D/5, Jim . . ." Armstrong said.

"Yes, Inspector?"

"I can't authorise this overtime. You'll have to take time off in lieu. You know the regulations, and overtime wasn't authorised for that Weymouth Mansions job . . ."

"I wouldn't have stayed overtime, Inspector, if Springer hadn't stuck his knife into me and that doctor hadn't kept me waiting in Casualty."

"I know, Jim. Don't think I don't sympathise. But you know the regulations."

"I'm already owed thirty-seven and a half days off in lieu."

"That makes two of us. The chief would never pass it."

Sergeant Boskin's voice was resigned. "Okay, Inspector, I'll make out another D/5."

Armstrong thought for a moment. "When you're making it out, Jim, you might like to include one item you've apparently forgotten. That taxi you took to the hospital to have that knife wound fixed . . ."

"Taxi, Inspector? You took me in your car!"

"Funny thing, Jim. I don't remember that. The regulations say you're permitted emergency transport if you're injured on duty, and I suppose a taxi qualifies . . ."

"Thanks, Inspector," Sergeant Boskin said.

Armstrong put down the telephone. Regulations were meant to be used, weren't they? The chuckle lasted all the way through the next six expense forms. Fate was kind to him that afternoon. When he started the seventh he heard the familiar rattle outside the door, which opened. Mrs. Tew put her head round it. "Hope you don't mind having your tea now, Inspector? I'm trying to get away early."

"What's the occasion?"

"Wonder of wonders. My old man's taking me out. So I'm going to have my hair done." She put a cup of tea on his desk. "I've got another outside for Inspector Pemberton, but I imagine you could find a home for it?"

Fate was indeed kind. It even permitted him to drink both cups before the telephone rang. "Armstrong . . . ?"

"Yes, Chief?"

"Word of warning about tonight. Don't let's have another of your cook-ups. Let's keep it simple, straightforward, uncomplicated. The divisional chief superintendent will be taking charge, so watch your step."

"Will you be there?"

"I wouldn't miss it. How are you getting on with that report on the Sturgis case?"

Armstrong glanced at the papers in the pending tray. Damn; he'd forgotten about the Sturgis report. "Nearly finished, Chief," he said, mentally crossing his fingers. The chief had a habit of saying, "Bring what you've done so far."

"I would have finished it," he said, "but you asked for the D/1 and D/5s."

"Ah, glad you reminded me. Bring them up right away, and I'll go through them with you."

"I haven't initialled all of them . . ."

"We can go through them together."

Oh, God, don't say it was going to be another of those days. A hundred things to do, and the chief wanted to concentrate on the one Armstrong knew would take time. He dialled the switchboard number. "I'll be with the chief inspector," he said.

"Hang on a second. We've got a call for you."

It was Sarah, his wife. "Make it quick, love," he said. "I'm on my way up to see the chief."

"Not in trouble again, are you?" she asked.

He laughed. "I do sometimes have to see him on routine matters."

"You can't tell me yet what time you'll be home?"

"I'm afraid not.

"Shall I take the kids to the shops. Save you the bother . . ."

"I've told you, love, I'll take care of it."

"But you've got so much on your plate. I just thought . . ."

"What's a husband for. . . . You know I enjoy doing things for you . . ."

"That girl Susan called again."

"What did she want?"

"She wouldn't say. Wouldn't even give me her name or leave a message, but I recognised her voice. Just, were you here, when would you be back, when would be a good time to ring you to catch you in . . . ?"

"How did she sound?"

"Hard to say. Bit upset, perhaps, a bit anxious."

"I've got to go, love. The chief's waiting."

Armstrong looked round the office, found a packet of manilla folders on the top of the filing cabinet, extracted one, and scrawled on the front "D/1s and D/5s AWAITING APPROVAL."

That would impress the chief.

At 6:28 the manager of the Royal Hall received a telephone call from Bill Simpson, the secretary of the Music Society of the nearby Students' Union.

"I hardly know how to tell you this, Mr. Barrett, but we've had a meeting this afternoon and I'm afraid a few hot-heads have forced through a motion calling for a demonstration against the Royal Hall. For banning the pop concert and substituting 'An evening with Beethoven.' "

"Oh dear," Mr. Barrett said, "we went into all that with the press at the time. The majority of our patrons is with us, you know, or we wouldn't be fully booked for the Beethoven, would we?"

"That's why I'm telephoning, Mr. Barrett. We're with you in principle . . ."

"I should jolly well hope you are. If you're going to waste our time with demonstrations outside the Hall I'm afraid I shall have to bring the matter of your concession tickets before the board of trustees."

"We don't want to lose that concession. The demonstration tonight won't last for long and there'll be absolutely no violence."

"What happens if a few extremists take over and our patrons are inconvenienced. Or even injured . . . ?"

"I've got help from members of the Rugger Club."

There was a pause while Mr. Barrett considered his position. Finally, he spoke. "Thank you for telephoning me, Mr. Simpson. Most civilised of you."

"I just wanted to let you know there was nothing to be bothered about," Bill Simpson said, as he hung up.

As soon as Bill Simpson had hung up, Barrett called the police station in Beacon Gardens and was put through to the chief inspector and identified himself.

"I usually talk to Superintendent Morris . . ."

"The superintendent's out, I'm afraid. Can I help you? Chief Inspector Roberts, C.I.D."

"Well, perhaps you can help me. You know there is to be a concert here this evening?"

"I didn't know personally, Mr. Barrett, but I expect they do downstairs. Do you require assistance . . . ?"

"I've just received a telephone call from a Mr. Simpson of the Music Society of the Students' Union. He told me that this evening a few students will be demonstrating outside the Hall."

"That was very civil of him. Do you want us to be there?"

"On the contrary. I don't want a fuss made. Mr. Simpson has promised there will be no violence."

"And is this Mr. Simpson in a position to honour that promise?"

"I think so."

"Then may I ask you, Mr. Barrett, why you're ringing the police?"

"Like you, Chief Inspector, I have to abide by a set of rules."

"But you're not asking for assistance?"

"On the contrary. I'm asking you not to intervene unless your set of rules compels you to do so. But I'd be grateful if you'd have a man standing by. Inconspicuously, of course."

"Of course, Mr. Barrett. I understand. We'll just keep our eyes open. After all, that's what the police are for, isn't it, to keep their eyes open . . . ?"

CHAPTER 1

"Lend me five, lover boy," Mary said, her hand high on my leg.

I looked at her. Did she think me that much of a sucker? "If you lend me five now, you can have it back, and anything you like upstairs afterwards. That's a promise, cross my heart."

I took five pounds from my wallet and made a mental note to remember to put it on my next D/1, hoping the chief would pass it. What an afternoon! I thought I'd never get away. If it had not been for this job, the chief would have kept me at it until the end of the shift, querying every item. I handed Mary the five pounds. "Come on," she said, "let's have a gamble."

The room was small and, contrary to the Gaming Act of 1970, contained a bar as well as a roulette table. No gaming licence, no liquor licence. I had checked. Harry, the owner (Harry the pimp as he was known to us), sat on a high stool at the head of the roulette table. It had been a good afternoon for the house, but you wouldn't guess that to look at his face. His eyes constantly picked at the room like those of a magpie, and he frowned when he saw the croupier slide five one pound chips to Mary, no doubt thinking she'd have done better to start with ten shilling chips to get the sucker—me—hooked. "I feel dead lucky today," Mary said. She spread her chips round the number seventeen, four splits, one straight up. The ball rolled round the wheel and dropped, and she gave a squeal of delight.

"I've done it," she said. "Seventeen. I've won. I told you I felt lucky." The croupier announced the winning number in an impassive voice that said, "Win or lose, it's all the same to me." The man they'd called Freeman had won eight pounds; the man who looked like a builder had lost twenty in ten shilling chips spread across the board and Harry smiled thinly. Mary clutched my arm saying, "I've won, I've won." The croupier paid Freeman, then raked a plaque across to Mary for one hundred pounds and a five pound chip. She slid the chip back to the croupier. "That's for you," she said, and scooped her bet off the seventeen. Five one pound chips. She handed them to me. "There you are," she said, "now don't say I don't keep my promises."

I glanced at my watch.

The builder had run out of money. "Stop gambling for today," Harry said, before the builder could ask for further credit. "Take Pat upstairs. On the house."

The time was seven twenty-nine and forty-five seconds.

I walked to the roulette table and in a loud clear voice said, "I am a police officer. Don't anybody move." I heard them rushing up the stairs outside. The door burst open and Sergeant Roper stood there, in uniform.

"It's a raid," one of the girls shrieked.

"You lousy pig," Mary shouted at me.

The next seconds were a confused blur of movement. Roper stepped forward into the room and a rash of constables appeared behind him. Freeman moved towards me. Harry started to slide backwards towards a curtain which doubtless concealed an emergency exit. He was clutching the cash box containing the afternoon's take. I swung round the top of the roulette table towards him. Freeman kept on moving towards me. The chief inspector came through the doorway behind the constables. The divisional chief superintendent appeared behind him. As I went round the top of the table, I momentarily lost my balance and flung out my right arm. The hard blade of my right hand connected with Freeman's throat in a karate chop. The constables grabbed Mary, Pat, and the two other girls who'd been in the room, and Freeman stopped dead, like a pole-axed bull. The chief inspector saw me apparently strike Freeman and he came forward but Freeman dropped to the carpet, out cold. I grabbed Harry's arm, the one holding the cash box. The divisional chief superintendent bent over Freeman, and when he straightened up he looked at the chief inspector and groaned, as if the blow had struck him.

"You know who this is, Chief Inspector?"

"Face is familiar, Chief Superintendent."

"It ought to be. He's Maurice Brigham, Member of Parliament."

The chief inspector shuddered. So did I.

"I just don't know what I'm going to do with you, Inspector Armstrong," the chief said to me, on the pavement outside the gambling club. "You heard who that man was? The one you hit?"

"Yes, Chief. Maurice Brigham. Member of Parliament. Got in at the last election with a large majority on a pledge to bring back law and order . . ."

"He's in Opposition, Armstrong, and even you should know what that means. He's a thorn in the side of the home secretary; and a pain in the arse to every copper on the police force. And you have to chop him across the throat . . ."

"It was an accident, Chief . . ."

"Everything's always an accident with you, Armstrong . . ."

"I was trying to stop the owner sliding out behind that

curtain. My arm swung through the air when I turned. Brigham moved forward, my hand met his throat. It could have happened to anybody . . ."

"It could only have happened to you, and only with a man like Brigham . . ."

"When we tell him it was an accident. . . ."

"You think he'll believe us . . . ? I'll take a bet he'll sue you for assault. . . . Even I can write the headlines. POLICE INSPECTOR ACCUSED OF REVENGE ASSAULT ON M.P., with a sneering editorial pointing yet again to police brutality."

"If I might say something, Chief. Serves him right for being in the place. A den of vice that is. Tarts, drugs I'm damn certain, out of hours drinking without a licence, gambling in contravention of the gaming laws. A bent wheel . . ."

The chief inspector laughed at me. "Maurice Brigham is scopic specimen tacked to a glass plate, a creepy crawly thing he wouldn't even touch with a spatula. "This was supposed to be a simple investigation. We all knew Harry was up to his old tricks again running a brothel, a gaming room on the side with a bent wheel. All we wanted from you was to be in there when the raid took place, to make certain nobody flashed a weapon, or hid any evidence. If you'd hit Harry nobody would have cared. But no, you had to hit Maurice Brigham, the one man who can make life hell for us . . ."

"He won't dare talk about his membership of a place like that. . . ."

The chief inspector laughed at me. "Maurice Birgham is a lay preacher and an opponent of the 'permissive society.' He's conducting a campaign against the police alleging that we're no better than the thugs we try to control. He says we lean on people too much, that we're bone-headed and use our fists when we ought to be using our brains. In your case, Armstrong, he could be right. Of course he was a member of that club, and he won't hesitate to tell the newspapers why. . . . In fact, that alone will get this story onto every front page. Why I joined the sin and sex club, by Maurice Brigham. Why do you think Maurice Brigham was in that club today? Because he fancied one of the dolly birds? Because he's got so much money he wanted to chuck it away on a bent wheel? He was there for exactly the same reason you were. He's on the same side we're supposed to be on, lad, the side of law and order. And that doesn't include chopping people on the throat . . ."

"I wasn't to know why he was there, Chief."

"You ought to have recognised his face. You must have seen his picture in the papers."

"I thought there was something familiar about him, but I identified him with Barney's race-course gang, the one that was doing Newmarket all last year. . . ."

It sounded lame, even to me. I ought to have recognised Brigham. Granted he was one of the new bunch and hadn't yet appeared on television, nor had his picture been often in the papers. But I ought to have recognised him and not assumed that because his face was somehow vaguely familiar he was a lag. Having recognised him, I could have done a good turn for the police by taking him on one side and showing him how well in control we were. It would have impressed him to know we didn't let slag like Harry get away with it. Good P.R., that would have been.

But me, I'm accident prone. No two ways about it. One time I was chasing a burglar in a stately home. I caught him and, though he was known to be rough, I brought him down with a flying tackle. But as I fell my foot touched a glass case on a pedestal. *My* foot, not the burglar's. The Ming vase in that case was valued at twenty thousand pounds before I got to it. When I left the stately home with my burglar, they were sweeping the Ming and the glass case into a dustpan, with a very small brush.

People were starting to come out of the club. Prostitutes, scalpers, policemen. Mary was one of the first and she spat when she saw me.

"Pig," she said, and turned to the chief inspector. "He was feeling me all over just before the raid," she said. "And talking dirty to me. Bloody pervert, that's what he is."

I was too sick of the whole business even to deny it.

"A pig and a sex-maniac, that's what he is," she went on. "You should have heard the things he was asking me to do to him . . ."

"Get on with you, Mary," the chief inspector said. "I was booking your mother thirty years ago when she was teaching Chinese sailors down at the dock gates. . . ."

Mary climbed into the wagon.

"Look lad," he said, "Brigham'll be out in a minute. Get back to the station and lose yourself for the rest of this shift. I don't know about you, I really don't. I send you out on the simplest assignment, and somehow it always becomes a balls-up. Cases that other inspectors can button up in half a day become a nightmare when you're handling 'em . . ."

"If that's an official complaint, Chief Inspector . . ."

"Don't get shirty, lad. Not with me. Get back to the station, write me out a full report of this incident, and then get lost. Until court time tomorrow. Understand? I don't want to see or talk to you until court time tomorrow."

"Very good, Chief Inspector."

As I walked away they opened the door of the wagon to push another girl inside. Mary was sitting at the back of the long side seat. "See you in court tomorrow," she said, "and wait 'til they hear what I have to tell them about you and your filthy habits. . . ."

It would sound all right in court. "I never touched her,

your honour," but somehow they never quite believe you, do they?

They never quite believe you, do they? Sarah, my wife, didn't quite believe me about Susan. She'd believed me at first, admired me even. Susan had been another of my "mistakes." She was eighteen the first time I picked her up. In Rose's café, with a bunch of greasers. Motorbikes parked outside, big jobs with chopper handlebars, flash chrome everywhere, and the exhaust pipes they call megas pointing up at the sky behind 'em. Cup of coffee, and think it's big to drop fifty newpence into the fruit machine, pour the tomato ketchup into the sugar bowl, and stick a hand up the waitress's skirt if she tries to wash the tabletop. I walked in there one Saturday afternoon. We'd had complaints from Rose, the manageress. She pointed to the biggest and burliest of them. "I'm not having it," she said. "I'm a respectable woman with kids."

Fred, his name was. I'd known him since he was an eight-year-old snot-nose, and the last ten years had done nothing for him. Hair I wouldn't wipe my feet on, down to his shoulders. Sweat shirt with HONDA written on it. Leather jacket with more brass than an old cannon. Scarf, once white silk, now the colour of a drunkard's eyes. The product of a system that says anyone who can get an erection is fit to be a father.

They were watching me. Ten of 'em. You either shit yourself or get stuck in. "Right," I said, "you. Outside."

He sneered, said nothing. His eyes spoke for him. "Make me, pig." He came upright as I went in, a lot of muscle and bone, but a lot of greasy café chips flesh. Grab his hand, turn his wrist, and his arm had to go down and back, and I pushed it so far up he could have hung his scarf on it. Eyes right and left. Tom starts to come in, side kick down his shins and he goes back howling. Mick on the other side, help his mates won't he, but a jab in his shoulder with the flat of my hand. "Watch it, baby-boy," and he collapsed back in the chair. Leaving me holding Fred, bloody great lummox of a lad, but I've got his arm up his back and my cobblers well out of his reach, and Rose, the respectable woman, has opened the door and I march him through it and with malice aforethought push him straight into that choppered Honda. He sprawls across it and down, bringing the bike off its stand and knocking a Yamaha down with it and he's a mess of tangled arms and legs and spokes and exhaust pipes. When the kids stream out of the café behind him, all they can think about is the bikes. "Knock it off, Fred, you've scratched my chrome."

Should have been the end of that scene. Cup of tea and a hamburger with Rose, maybe. Respectable woman, indeed, with kids! The current price was three quid on a sofa upstairs, above the café, but the young lads wouldn't know about that, would they? They could get all they wanted free.

One face I'd not seen before. I grabbed her arm. "You," I said, "not so fast. Back inside." There were jeers. "Look at the pig, after a bit of nooky . . ." but I was used to that. Some people think the only reason you bother with the young girls is so you can feel 'em up. She sat down at a table near the back.

"Up here," I said, "where everybody can see us."

Her name was Susan. She'd just moved to London from Leeds. We could check that.

Honest, from Crossgates in Leeds.

Run away?

No, just walked out.

Broken home?

No, just an utter and complete drag.

Father strict, eh?

Not him; he never knew I existed. TV and the Buffs, that's my Dad.

And your Mum goes to bingo?

How did you know?

They all do. Short of love, were you?

Love. A dirty word, that is. Didn't ask to be born, did I? Didn't choose them for parents, did I?

Put your handbag on the table, open it, and turn it upside down. How old are you?

Eighteen.

Silly cow had five. In a plastic box. Where did you get them? Do you smoke them?

I sell them.

Silly cow. That makes you a pusher.

I don't touch drugs.

What are these?

You can't get addicted on reefers, anybody knows that. Not like drugs.

Go on then. Tell me, what are drugs?

Alcohol. Tobacco. Heroin. LSD. Things like that.

You never heard of marijuana? Cannabis resin?

Yes, but they're not drugs, are they? You can't get hooked on mari, can you?

Same old story. Where did you go to school, love?

St. Agatha's Convent, Crossgates.

Pass any exams?

I tried for two O-levels.

Daft question. Did you get them? No, of course she didn't. Put her inside and the first person who talked to her would recommend a plea of diminished responsibility.

Parents, bloody parents. I have two kids, a boy twelve and a girl eleven. They know about cannabis, know how it can lead to drug dependence, which can lead to drug addiction. They know about accepting lifts or gifts from unknown men, going for walks in woods to pick wild flowers.

But Susan didn't. At eighteen. Same old story. Parents have a kid, pay money to send it to a "good" school, and forget that home is where most of the difficult things of life are learned. But if they're paying a few pounds a term they think they can absolve themselves of responsibility every time they write a cheque. Susan was eighteen. I would say she had the mental age of a kid of twelve. In every sense of the word, she was innocent. She had no guile, no dissimulation, no malice, no avarice, no envy, no false pride.

That's when I made my first mistake with Susan. I ought to have cautioned her, marched her straight to the station with Rose as a witness I hadn't touched the girl, booked her, and left her to my superiors.

But I didn't. I believed her, and thought I could help her.

"Where do you get these reefers?"

"A lad. I don't know his name."

"Where do you meet him?"

"He comes to the 101; that's a snack bar on Springfield Street."

"I know what the 101 is, love. It's a den of thieves. Look, Susan, you're doing a bad thing smoking those reefers, and you're doing an even worse thing selling 'em. Now I want you to promise me you won't buy any more of them, or smoke any more, but above all I want you to promise you won't sell any more . . ."

"A policeman, aren't you?" she said.

"Yes, a detective."

"Are you going to arrest me?"

"Not if you promise to do as I ask."

I stayed with her in Rose's until it was time to go to the 101. Her contact didn't show so I saw her home. She was living in digs in Martin's Mount. "Come and see me in the morning when you get up," I said, "and I'll see if I can get you a job."

"You're very nice to me," she said, and quite instinctively she stumbled forward and tried to thank me the only way she knew how, by kissing me. Luckily I turned my face away, but unluckily her lips brushed against my collar. She wasn't wearing much lipstick, but enough. Sarah, my wife, believed me. That time.

The duty cars were busy outside Harry's club; it was only a four-minute walk to the station. The open forecourt of the Royal Hall was a seething mass of people as I walked past. The usual cars drew up outside the door and discharged the usual herd of sleek animals, and I felt my usual stab at the sight of them. I can't help myself, but there's something about overt wealth and what I believe they call "conspicuous consumption" that switches me right off. I suppose I see too much of the other side, the inconspicuous but mean poverty.

Other people were arriving quietly in taxis or walking from the bus stop or crossing the road after a stroll in the park, and I longed to be with them, free of mental turmoil, enjoying a quiet satisfying evening listening to the music I like. I had an uncle who was a cellist in an orchestra; he was the one who introduced me to the classics. It's always been one of my regrets I never learned to play a violin. There's nothing I'd like better than to sit in an orchestra, holding a violin in my hands. But my parents were stuck on security, and it was a bank, the post office or the police force for me, with the pension held out as the top of Everest. I'd been to high school, had done well enough to have no difficulty about a job, but I'd missed a scholarship that would have taken me on to university. Dad's wages behind the counter of a men's clothing store didn't allow for dreams.

A student demonstration was in full spate, and automatically my eye searched for somebody from uniformed branch. Jenkins was standing across the road, apparently minding his own business, with his radio clipped to his lapel ready to call for assistance if the demonstration became violent.

The demonstrators were the usual long-haired bunch. Too easy to say they're unwashed and unkempt. Kids don't care about external appearance anymore, and I don't see why they should. Provided they don't threaten persons or property, or obstruct the Queen's highway, or cause an unlawful affray. Okay, so I'm inclined to be permissive, and cops are supposed to be reactionary. But I've had a lot of long-haired lads in the station and I've talked to them and often provocation has been the direct cause of any petty infringement they may have done. How's that for a copper talking? How's that for one of your brutal pigs? Mark you, I hate the layabouts like poison, and thump them hard. The students carried the usual posters; this time the slogans read BEETHOVEN IS DEAD, WHAT ABOUT THE LIVING MUSIC?

My eyes flicked round again, looking for the professional agitators, the commie go-anywhere disrupt-anything fanatics, who'll support any cause as long as it means the downfall of our society. Oh yes, we have them on our patch. They make a living at it. Don't ask me who pays them, but they don't do any work. Just organise demonstrators that bit further than they intended to go, so that what starts as a peaceful walk becomes a stone-throwing, bottle-chucking riot. Then the professionals quietly go home.

Two beefy students stood on the pavement, their eyes wary. The demonstrators were walking in an orderly crocodile back and forwards along a path of which the two students were the end markers. The two at the end were wearing blazers, shirts, ties, and grey flannel slacks. I could see three more dressed the same way. They had the wide shoulders and the stocky bearing of rugby players and I could tell that, whatever the demonstrators might think, the blazers were in charge.

No commissionaires about, no sign of the manager.

If Jenkins couldn't cope, he knew what to do. Meanwhile, he was being sensible, playing it cool, by staying right out of it.

The better part of valour is discretion.

~

Some coppers learn discretion; I never have. I ought to have stayed right out of it with Susan. I probably would have done, if I hadn't had two kids of my own. If they hadn't been coming on so well at school. Bright as a couple of buttons. My girl, Helen, was form captain, and my boy, though too irresponsible to be made a prefect, was a man's lad. Played football and cricket for the teams, usually came about middle in the form with an invariable note from the headmaster, "could do better if he put his back into it." We'd have a mock row about it, once a term, and I'd threaten to cut off his pocket money, knowing full well Sarah would make it up to him, and for a few weeks his nose would go down, and he'd do well. But then he'd slip back again. I didn't mind. He was very nice to Sarah, and looked after his sister.

Susan ought to have had a brother. And she ought to have had parents who cared enough to give her a sensible education, instead of leaving her in the hands of fluttering convent sisters whose only ideas of reality were the mortification of your knees on hard prayer boards and emptying your plate at meal times. I asked Susan, once, if she'd had any sex education. Oh yes. Once, Sister Brigit came in and said, "Today we're going to have sex education, and I'm going to tell you all about men's funny little ways. . . ."

I got her a job. In a shop. They fired her after a week. She couldn't add up. I got her another. Wrapping parcels in a large store. She lasted three weeks. Half the parcels went astray. She had no visual memory. She'd read 15 Wayby Place on the shipping advice and write 51 Wayby Terrace on the label.

But she had a lovely smile and you couldn't be cross with her. "Not very good at it, am I?" she said.

"We can't all be good at everything."

She was a wonderfully open girl, good-looking, a treat to be with. You could read her feelings from her face, when you weren't looking at it to think how pretty she was. A very rare person, no malice, no bitchiness—alas, not much intelligence either, but a sense of humour that made up for that and an honesty about admitting her mistakes. She had no knowledge of conventional right and wrong. She based her life on an instinctive desire not to hurt anyone's feelings. She was interested in everything, bright as a button, full of enthusiasms, but she treated everything as it came. The present was too alive, too vibrant, for her to think of things gone and things to come. There was no point in arranging a meeting for a certain time because she had no sense of time. She'd start out to meet me and on the way she'd see something interesting and follow it, and then see something more interesting and follow that, and forget all about her original intentions of coming to meet me. I tried hard to get her to fit into the normal way of life. To do things as other people did them. But every time I made one of those absurd generalisations about the way other people live, she'd cock her head and say, "Do you really think so?" as if she was surprised the lives of other people were important to me. Susan hadn't been given any rules of conduct and did whatever came naturally to her. From her own innocence. That might work in an ideal society, but in the corrupt cess-pit that commercial interests have made of modern life, she couldn't survive for long. Unless I could help her see the evil about her and the need for self-discipline.

She'd stopped going out with the greasers. She now kept herself neat and tidy. Imitating me, I suppose. She didn't smoke reefers so far as I knew. Didn't smoke or drink. I don't smoke or drink spirits but I learned the hard way. When I smoke I cough, and when I drink anything but beer I get drunk and vomit. She didn't need artificial stimulation. But she had no sense of conventional morality. She'd ride fifteen stops on a tube train without a ticket and pay only for a journey from the next station. She'd ride on a bus and when the conductor came for the fare she'd ask for a destination in the other direction then get off the bus in pretended confusion. Two such rides and she'd arrive where she wanted to be without paying any fare. Once I took her into a supermarket. I had to get a few things for Sarah. When we came out, Susan showed me the things in her pocket. "Why did you bother to pay?" she asked me. "They weren't watching." Being with her was like standing beside an unexploded bomb. I took her back into the supermarket and we showed them the goods and paid for them. When we came out the second time she pouted at me as if I'd spoiled her game. "You must be crazy," she said. "I didn't want half this stuff anyway."

It took a whole evening to go through "thou shalt not steal," not even hair shampoos you don't want. How could I, without getting into a difficult argument about possessions and possessiveness, explain to someone who says "whoever owns that place is a rich man and won't miss it." I was in no position to argue that issue; personally I hate tradesmen and shopkeepers; I hate their vicious mean grasping ways, extracting the last penny from the customers they mostly despise. Any copper will tell you, never ask a shopkeeper to take it easy on a thief. Sure, the old lady's nicked a small loaf and a tin of sardines, but if she'd got them home to eat, they'd have been the only food till the post office paid out the pensions. But try telling that to a shopkeeper.

Finally, I only had one argument. "Susan," I said, "take my word for it, and don't steal . . ."

"Because it's wrong . . . ?"

"Thats right, because it's wrong, and it hurts me when you do it."

She grabbed hold of my arm, and hugged me as we walked along. The shopping bag weighed a ton, but I didn't mind.

"I don't want to do anything to hurt you," she said.

"Susan, love," I said, "trust me and believe me. Promise me you won't take anything from supermarkets, or any other shop, without paying for it."

She promised and, what was flattering to me, she kept her promise. I began to hope I was communicating with her. If she said she wouldn't do something, she didn't. If she said she would do something, she did. And I made the decisions. To do, or not to do. For me, it was like drawing a blueprint of my ideal person and that's a dangerous seductive ability. A Svengali, with his Trilby. But I rationalised what I was doing by believing she'd started to accept the existence of a moral code, a set of values, and once she'd done that she'd work out her own special interpretation of it.

I didn't see that she was gradually becoming dependent on me, that my thoughts were her thoughts, my values her values. Sarah tried to point that danger out to me, I can see that now, but I told myself the method didn't matter so long as it achieved results. Susan was a sheet of white paper on which anyone could write. The greasers had written reefers there, petty theft, and contempt for authority. I'd managed to erase that, and start fresh.

It was my one success, during a time of my life when I

was conscious of so many failures. It would be easy now to say I'd needed Susan as much as she'd needed me.

I got her a job looking after four young kids whose mum was pregnant again and had to keep popping in and out of a hospital bed for blood tests. Nothing to add up, nothing to write, just four tots to feed, wash, dress up, and take out in the park. Like playing at dolls with the walking talking models. Playing with them on the rug she was in a seventh heaven. Saving money too, since it was a live-in job. But then the master of the house, a randy bastard who'd made his wife pregnant every year of the marriage so far, climbed into bed with her. As innocently as she'd told me she was selling reefers, she told the man's wife she was sleeping with him. And that's when I discovered she had no inhibitions about sleeping with anybody. So long as they were decent to her.

"Didn't the nuns tell you about venereal disease and pregnancy while they were telling you about 'men's funny little ways'?" I asked her.

She shook her head. Dammit, she was eighteen.

When I'd seen what was going on outside the Royal Hall, and knew that Jenkins, one of our more senior and sensible coppers, was keeping an efficient and unobtrusive eye on it, I carried on back to the station. It's in one of those new buildings along Ken High Street, all glass and concrete. I like it that way; it's more efficient than the old-fashioned Victorian buildings most coppers are housed in. I nodded hello to the desk sergeant who was busy taking details of what sounded like a missing lover but was, in fact, a lost dog. I climbed the stairs to our office on the first floor, since the lift was up on the fourth floor. I sat at my desk, drew the typewriter forward, and started to write notes for an account of the Maurice Brigham affair. Pemberton was still out on his inquiries and the room had the peaceful evening feeling, that calm before the storm of pub-closing mayhem.

But then something happened to make me forget the Maurice Brigham affair; and that's what the rest of this story is all about. I'm going to set it down in chronological order, because that's the way the chief likes to read things. A lot of it is "after-acquired knowledge," a lot of it is hearsay and wouldn't, of course, be acceptable in a court. But I'll try to write it more or less as it happened, or as I was later told it had happened.

CHAPTER 2

So we start in the Royal Hall. This part of the story takes seventy-one minutes, the time taken to perform the Beethoven Ninth Symphony. All the seats had been sold, and the Hall was full to capacity, but I'll go back a few minutes. . . .

When the commissionaires started to close the doors of the Royal Hall a few minutes before eight o'clock, the demonstrators stacked their banners neatly inside the entrance to be collected later, repainted with some new slogan and used on the next protest. They drew their tickets from Bill Simpson, and climbed in orderly fashion up to the Gods. The non-demonstrators had saved seats for them on the benches and they filed in and sat behind the rail. Several produced mini-scores of the music and opened them at the first page. One girl produced a clarinet part, took her clarinet from its case, assembled it without a reed, and sat with her fingers limbering up, ready to follow the music without actually blowing the notes.

The manager was standing at the side of the rostrum, beaming at all and sundry. The concert manager had checked that everyone had his music. The union secretary had collected a few last-minute subs, the tympanist had tuned his instruments.

Otto Flughafer was lying flat on his back, mentally reading the score. This would be the first time he'd conducted a major work with a major orchestra and a large choir in public, in the holy of holies, the Royal Hall.

No one was paying any attention to the judge sitting in a box absolutely still, from long practice, ready to listen to anything that might be placed before him before passing judgement.

No one paid any attention to the man on the fourth seat of the first row in the second block of the auditorium, the man with a black bag on his knee which, from time to time, he fingered nervously. The expression on his face would be hard to read accurately. Concealed triumph? An inner defiance, a now-I've-got-them-all kind of superiority. That's hindsight on my part.

Another man sitting near the front was also carrying a black bag but his was smaller and bore the marks of constant use.

Every seat taken except for a few in the members' boxes. Orchestra sitting, choir sitting, audience buzzing with the anticipation that precedes any performance of any musical work, the sort of thrill you don't get from a phonograph record, the feeling of being where it's all going to happen.

Notices had been posted all round the concert hall saying the concert would start on time and latecomers would not be admitted until the interval. For once the public had responded and, as the last door closed at eight o'clock, Pierre Faugeras came on and received his usual enthusiastic welcome. He was a well-known and well-loved musician and the Paris State Symphony Orchestra under his leadership had been conducted by such legendary figures as Toscanini and Beecham. Otto Flughafer walked onto the platform at exactly one minute past eight, bowed curtly to his somewhat restrained ovation, turned his back on the crowd, as if they weren't there, raised his baton, and brought it down for the music to start. It was a strictly no-nonsense beginning.

As soon as James Barrett heard the music begin he went into his private office. The demonstration had given him a few bad minutes, but he had not intervened nor, thanks to his telephone call to the chief inspector, had the police. The students, he'd been relieved to note, were merely letting off steam. Now, seventy minutes of blessed relaxation stared him in the face, and stronger men than he have failed to resist that particular temptation. He unbuttoned his "uniform" dinner jacket, selected a cigarette, lit it as carefully as if it were a Havana cigar, and sat down.

He told himself he'd been right to cancel the "pop" part of the concert, right to offer his patrons "An Evening with Beethoven." Of course, many people had come merely to watch Otto Flughafer make a fool of himself. Perhaps the programme should have been less demanding. Tchaikovsky, perhaps, or Grieg . . . but these young conductors had to make a start sometime, and he'd certainly filled the house, for whatever reason.

A white envelope lay on his table. He hadn't noticed it there before. He leaned forward idly, picked it up, opened it, and read the message on the folded sheet of paper it contained.

AT THE END OF THE CHORAL SYMPHONY, YOU'LL HAVE A DEATH ON YOUR HANDS.

The words had been printed with a ballpoint pen and the sheet of paper looked as if it had been torn from a pad to judge from the line of gum at its head. What a wretched bore. Just when he was about to relax . . . an anonymous note at this time of evening. What a bore.

A competent administrator has a mind like a computer, with each possible circumstance having its own check list of actions. What to do if a cleaner falls down and breaks a leg . . . a musician arrives without his instrument . . . there are complaints the hall is too hot/cold. The check list for anonymous notes began: First ensure the note is handled as little as possible. He put the note on the table next to the envelope. He got up, walked across the cupboard in which he kept his overcoat, took out his soft unlined leather gloves, and put them on. Only then did he glance at his wrist-watch. The time was two minutes past eight. He opened the secretaire, drew forward the day book in which he kept notes for future reports, and wrote in it, "Anonymous note discovered, two minutes past eight."

James Barrett was not the man to curse, even to himself, but he permitted himself a feeling of intense irritation. "Bill Simpson said nothing about an anonymous note," he thought. This really was carrying the joke too far. The demonstration itself had been bad enough, and thank God it had taken place without violence, but an anonymous note —really, that was too bad, that was going too far.

Now it had all been put in writing, now it was an official matter. Letters, even anonymous ones, had a demanding existence. You couldn't just ignore a letter. He made a note in the day book, writing neatly despite the handicap of leather gloves. "Speak to board re concession tickets for students."

It really was too bad of them to send it in writing.

During his tenure of office at the Royal Hall he had received many anonymous notes. All the concert halls were bothered with them from time to time. When the switchboard girl came on the telephone he deliberately kept his voice as unemotional, as undramatic, as possible. "Get me the local police station, will you, Annie?"

The police took the call at 2004 hours. At least, I logged it on my pad at that time. A good many things go on to a detective inspector's pad, and many of 'em, due to pressure of other crimes, other businesses, never come off it again.

This one did. I was bored, the chief inspector had told me to get lost, and I like Beethoven. I'd looked enviously at those posters when I'd passed the Royal Hall, but had no valid reason for going there. The demonstration was being "contained" by Jenkins; anyway, it wasn't an inspector's job.

I pressed the switch on the intercom and after getting a blast of static whine in my head I could hear the faint voice of our admin sergeant.

"Anything doing, Sergeant?"

"Bit early yet, Inspector."

"I've got something. Over at the Royal Hall. I was thinking of going over . . ."

"That demo? The chief's put a blanket on that one. Said to hold off until we got a specific request for assistance. Jenkins from uniformed branch has reported in saying the kids have all packed up and gone inside to listen to the music. I could pull him back off his beat to go and take a look if you like . . . ? Is it a 'request for assistance'?"

"No, an anonymous note . . ."

"Oh, one of them. Bloody students. Too much time on their hands. . . . Shall I pull Jenkins off the beat to look at it, not that I imagine there's anything in it."

Since the modernisation we've given all the beat men a walkie-talkie, and can get in touch with any one of them instantly. More and more men on the beat are being used to replace detectives, and that's something I don't approve of. The last thing I wanted was to have my possible evening's entertainment squandered on a copper on the beat slipping into the Royal Hall for a quick cuppa, on the excuse of checking out a story. Anonymous notes are a penny a dozen, but it would take Jenkins an hour to find out there was nothing in it. And I could use that hour, listening to Beethoven, making up my mind once and for all whether to jack it in or not, to tell the chief inspector I agreed with him I wasn't fit to run the public lavatories at a football ground.

"Since there's nothing going on, I think I'll go over myself and sniff around."

The sergeant chuckled through the static on the intercom, but he knew me well enough to take that liberty. He was a fellow sufferer. "Of course, the fact they're playing that classical music you're so keen on wouldn't have anything to do with your decision to go over there personally, would it, Inspector?"

I knew there were a dozen things I should be doing—the silver job, the M.O.T. test certificate job, clearing the expense vouchers the chief had thrown out, but I couldn't stomach the sight of that office anymore, now that the thought of an hour's peace had come.

I chuckled, too. "Look in the book, Sergeant. What to do in case of an anonymous note. I'll bet they've forgotten to amend it. 'In the event of the receipt of an anonymous note, the senior officer available will conduct an investigation as follows . . .' "

"That means, and you know it, Inspector, that first he'll send a copper round to take a quick butcher's . . ."

"I know what it means, Sergeant, and so do you, but that's not what it says. How In interpret 'conduct an investigation' is my own affair. I'm a big boy now . . ."

"Is that what I shall say to the chief inspector when he calls in asking for you? Inspector Armstrong presents his compliments, Chief, but says he's a big boy now . . ."

"Less than half an hour ago, the chief inspector told me to get lost . . ."

"Been at it again, Inspector. What was it this time . . . ?"

"Assault and battery, if I'm lucky . . ."

"I can see why you favour the Royal Hall. Pity we can't find an Interpol job for you, quickly. In somewhere like Zambia . . ."

Going towards the Royal Hall made me think of Susan again: I'd suggested once that I might take her to a concert with me, but somehow we'd kept putting it off.

After the nursemaid job, I got Susan a job at a hospital. Ward orderly. Making beds, helping the nurses and physiotherapists turn the patients over. She liked it; they put her on the kids' ward and she loved kids. It was a live-in job, a hostel with strict rules and fifty other females. I thought she'd make friends her own age and start a normal life again.

I was wrong.

Eleven o'clock one night, Sarah and I had deliberately gone to bed early. I'd been off duty all day and we'd taken the kids down to Hythe. We'd even dreamed about finding a derelict cottage and doing it up for my eventual retirement. Sarah goes along with a man's dreams, doesn't make him feel foolish the way some women do, with their feet so firmly stuck on the ground they leave an imprint with every backward step they take. The telephone rang. "Tell them you're off duty," Sarah said, knowing how often I'd said that before and still spent all night chasing villains.

It was Susan.

I hadn't talked to her for a few days and pleasure showed in my voice to judge from the look Sarah gave me.

"Can I see you, right away?" Susan asked.

Sarah must have heard; our bed isn't all that big and I wasn't being furtive.

"I'm in bed, love. It's gone eleven."

"You said to call any time."

"Yes, and I meant it. But I *am* in bed. Did you want anything special, or can it wait till tomorrow?"

"Don't mind me," Sarah said. We'd been together all day. She'd made a special supper. For once, the kids hadn't hung around. No one had to get up early in the morning.

"You said to ring," Susan said, in that child's voice I was beginning to recognise. "I need to see you. . . ."

Sure, I'd said to ring. "If anybody offers you reefers, or tries to get you into bed . . . there's my number, any time night or day . . ."

"All right. I'll meet you at the Wimpy in ten minutes." Sarah's back was already turned towards me as I got out of bed, pulled on a pair of trousers and a polo-necked sweater.

Susan was waiting when I got there. "What's the trouble?"

"This medical student. He keeps pestering me."

"Tell him to get lost . . ."

"It's difficult. I fancy him. He's very nice. . . ."

Dammit, mentally she was a kid of twelve. My Helen got the same look on her face when she wanted something and I had to say she couldn't have it. "Look, Susan, I fancy my wife. She's 'very nice.' But I left her in bed to come to see you. All right, so you fancy this medical student. All right, so he's very nice. But I've told you over and over again that you can't live your life from bed to bed, and that's what will happen if you don't watch it."

The door of the Wimpy Bar opened and let in a gust of clean and wholesome night air. Six people came in, three men and three women. All pissed. Big night out somewhere. "Look darling a Wimpy Bar, and it's still open. How quaint. Let's have a wimpy." Voices like buzz saws. "How absolutely decadent." Suddenly I laughed, remembering a story Sergeant Williamson had told me, about a titled lady who went on her honeymoon and in the middle of the act of consummation looked up at her new husband. "Is this what the ordinary people call 'fucking?'" "I suppose it must be, my dear . . ." "Then all I can say is that it's far too good for them . . ."

"What are you laughing at?" Susan asked.

"A joke somebody told me . . ."

"I know a joke. Shall I tell it to you. "It's a bit . . . you know."

"Then keep it to yourself . . ."

"What did they do when they found the nun was having a baby . . . ?"

"I said, keep it to yourself."

"They fired the canon. The cannon, get it?"

I must have laughed too loud, trying hard. A couple of people at a table to our right looked at me, as if I were laughing at them. Long hair, beads, amulets to ward off the evil conformity. They picked up headphones, placed them on their ears, and plugged into a cassette tape-recorder. "Good-bye cruel world, we're off to join the circus."

The Wimpy Bar was filled with problem people. People with nothing to do and nowhere to go to find someone to do it with. Tired hard men behind the counter fried meat and onions in an oil that seemed to cling to your clothes like yesterday's sweat. All ages. Old men we'd book for vagrancy to protect them from the cold night air, needlessly keeping them alive for further misery. Young men looking for a way of life, or a reason to continue to live it. Bright young things, late stop-outs, morning sleepers, whose parents' pittance kept them from facing a cold hard reality of nine to five employment. At the next table, a kid of forty, young after his time, shuffled through a sheaf of pages from a pad, muttering rhyme- and rhythm-less poetry. Occasionally he'd produce a ballpoint pen and change a word as if it mattered. Practised eye all around. None of my customers.

I had to talk to Susan all night, backwards and forwards along the same subject, feeling like a politician trying to justify his party point of view. How do you justify banning reefers to a kid as you offer them a cigarette with a cancer warning on the packet? How do you differentiate between the high of the reefered poet on the next table and the loutish drunken behaviour of the social high flyers on the table beyond, one of whom had just gone out to be sick—

poor George, he's icky boo—against the wall. How do you explain that a man doesn't need love to take his wife to bed on a Saturday night, provided he has the sanction of a minority cult called religion; if he becomes dissatisfied with the results he can either have a state-arranged abortion or pay someone to tell the minimum of truth to a divorce judge who will call the whole thing off.

"We wouldn't be harming anybody else, just doing it together . . ." Susan said. How can you explain that promiscuity causes an internal illness, poisoning your self-respect where no remedial treatment can reach.

So I fell back on the old mumbo-jumbo. "Look, Susan, trust me. I've had more experience of life than you have, and believe me, what I say is right. There'll come a time when you'll be old enough to appreciate that what I'm saying is for your own good." Bullshit of course, and what it lacked in logic I tried to express—like all politicians—by the tone of my voice.

I kept on talking until it was time for the nice medical student to go back on duty.

When I arrived home Sarah made my breakfast, and the kids' breakfast, and saw them off to school with her usual thousand injunctions. That's the way some people express love, by telling other people what not to do. It's as good a method of being a mother, or a copper, as any.

"Are you going to be all right?" she asked me. "Can you stay home today to have a couple of hours . . . ?"

I didn't need to go on duty until two o'clock so I slept the rest of the morning. "You take too much on yourself," Sarah said, when she brought me a cup of tea in bed and kissed me. Was that only a month ago?

It wasn't worth taking a duty car, so I walked fast to the Royal Hall, arriving at 2007 hours, six minutes after the start of the Beethoven Ninth. The manager, as we had arranged on the telephone, met me at the front entrance. First impressions not good. A prissy bastard, a professional administrator. Trying too hard to stay "with it"; longish sideboards, but the back of his hair well above his collar, a too stylish evening dress coat with a large tie in some velvet material; a black cummerbund in shot silk; nothing actually wrong with the way he looked but somehow the effect was less than the sum of all his parts. And trendy middle-aged men switch me off anyway. His eyes were sombre, but I imagined they'd been composed into something suited to the occasion, the panjandrum dealing with the small inconsequential affairs of the common people. Of whom, I could see in his eyes, I was definitely one. . . .

I approved of the gloves he wore, but didn't approve of him carrying the note with him. I didn't take the note seriously of course, any more than he did. For him it was a bore, for me a convenient excuse to get out of the station.

The music followed me all the way along the corridor to his office. When this sick world is laid to its final resting place, when the scientists blow us off the face of it, or the lying politicians deceive us into total war with each other, or business interests cheat and rob us into starvation, the sounds of classical music played by a symphony orchestra led and disciplined by a man like Faugeras, inspired by a good conductor, will continue to soar round this galaxy as the final epitaph to a man's ability to create beauty. Though, dammit, no one will be left to hear it. I get these fanciful ideas sometimes. We went into the manager's office. One thing I'll give him credit for; he'd had the sense to install a good loudspeaker system in the corner, and we could hear the music as plainly and as distortion-free as if we were in the Hall itself. Two original Bratbys on the wall, savage with splashes of a thickened ochre paint that made them leap out of the frames. Originals, not prints. A sculptured figure on a tabletop, long and thin in some kind of marble symbolising life or death or some such sublime subject made trivial in a sculptor's hands. Acres and acres of Times Furnishing Ltd. best green haircord, and a modern oval stone on a plinth with a hole carved in it. The stone, not the plinth. It could have been done by Henry Moore, or picked up on the sea-shore.

"May I know your name, sir?" I'm always polite, to start with.

"James Barrett."

"And you are the manager?"

"Of course."

He and the chief inspector would get on well together. "Can you please tell me how the note came into your possession?" Still dead polite. He'd put the note on the table. It bent open. Without touching it I read the wording on it. Next to it was the envelope in which it had come. The paper of the note and the envelope appeared commonplace.

"I found it here in my office." He said that as if it were a dog turd, which it was, of course, to him.

"When?"

"At two minutes past eight o'clock. I called you immediately."

I bent over and sniffed the note. No trace of perfume. There never is. The wording had been printed in block capitals, using a ballpoint pen. They sell a million ballpoint pens every day. We'd find out who made the paper, who made the envelope, who made the ballpoint pen. But how would that help us? Anybody can go into a Rymans and buy it. Anonymous notes used to be written on pads bought in Woolworth's, using letters cut out of the newspaper, but not anymore.

"Who has access to this office?"

He ignored the question. "I was surprised when you said you were coming over. A detective inspector. They don't usually bother, or if they do a constable comes. . . ." He was looking down his nose at me, as if despising me for demeaning myself by accepting the work of a constable.

"Yes, well, all our constables are busy with serious crime . . ."

"And you think this is frivolous . . . ?"

Good, I'd got him rattled. "Can't be 'frivolous,' can it? Or you wouldn't have wasted our time by telephoning. You've asked for assistance, Mr. Barrett, and you're entitled to the best you can get. Believe me, we shall spare no effort . . ."

Now his smile was sickly, like a man who's forgotten to put on the handbrake and watches his car roll down a slope into a wall.

"I'm only carrying out my instructions, Inspector."

"And I am only carrying out mine, Mr. Barrett. This note will be handed over to the forensic chaps and believe me they'll take it apart. Before they've finished with it we shall know all there is to know about the paper, the envelope, the pen used for the writing. It's a mammoth task, but they'll work at it night and day until they can give us the information we need . . ."

Yes, he definitely looked sickly. "I can probably tell you all that without your chaps being bothered," he said.

"You mean the students? The ones demonstrating here tonight?"

He nodded. "It really is no more than a student prank, Inspector," he said. "I only telephoned to comply with my instructions . . ."

"Are you prepared to lay evidence against one particular student?"

"Good Lord, no . . ."

"We could get him for breaking and entering . . ."

"Good Lord, I didn't think anything along those lines . . ."

"That's the trouble, Mr. Barrett, people don't. . . ." I was enjoying myself. The biter bit. The underdog who suddenly barks.

Otto Flughafer was making a cracking job of the Beethoven; and the strings under Faugeras . . . I'd never heard anything like 'em. I walked over to the door. There were no signs of forcible entry, but I didn't let that deter me. I opened and closed the door a couple of times, looked intently at the lock. Any one of a dozen firms makes them in Willenhall. Retail cost less than a pound; any one of my lads could open it with a bent paperclip.

"Do you always keep this door locked?" I knew he would; he was the type, and it was that sort of office, straight from Ideal Offices Exhibition.

"Always." Shock in his voice, as if I'd accused him of not keeping his flies closed.

"Who has the key?"

"I have."

"Does your secretary have a duplicate?"

"Of course not . . ." Why "of course"? Some people trust their secretaries. But not him.

"Does *anybody* have a key?" I knew very well who had the keys, and ticked them off, one by one, on my fingers. "The cleaners?"

"Yes."

"The nightwatchman?"

"Yes."

"The firemen, the day security men, the board of trustees, and probably half a dozen other people, if the truth is known."

His face blanched as he realised, probably for the first time, how many people had access to his sanctum. It would be hopeless to speculate how the note got on his table; more keys would open his office than a Woolworth's suitcase.

"No sign of anything missing, no disturbance? Anything not in its proper place? Anything at all?"

He hadn't checked. "I never thought of that," he said. Now he would think of it. It would nag him, worry him until he could get rid of me and check. He was looking round the room. His memory would recall anything of an orderly nature. He had that sort of mind, I would say. But he wouldn't recognise anything out of the ordinary. Few people do. It takes a detective to ask himself questions.

"No, there's nothing out of the ordinary," he said.

I walked down the corridor towards the body of the Hall, along one side of the long horseshoes and past the entrances to the private members' boxes. The sound of that gorgeous music, of course, was everywhere. I was revelling in it, going through the motions of an investigation. I looked into a couple of boxes through the small glass panel let into the door. Actually, I was looking for a seat myself.

The second box was empty; I opened the door quietly, and went in. The full volume of the orchestra came at me, warm and comforting as a hot bath. I sat down and let it engulf me.

What did it matter that I thought the manager a creep? What did it matter I'd hit Maurice Brigham in the throat and they were out there gunning for me. The Royal Hall was full of sound, and for a while I could relax in the sheer pleasure of it, deferring those fruitless speculations about my future. Let's face it, I wasn't really cut out to be a copper, was I? Oh, I was eager enough, too bloody eager they said, and efficient enough. But all the time I let myself become personally involved. Take Barrett for instance. It wasn't his fault I found him cold and bloodless. We can't all be instantly warm, instantly passionate. The world needs a few Barretts about, men who quietly and dispassionately get on with their jobs, making no fuss or bother, just doing what they have to do according to well-tried rules.

He'd followed me into the box, but for a moment I ignored him. The orchestra was playing like men possessed. It's impossible to describe playing in words, to set down that silky precision of a good string section thinking and bowing as one man, each instrument reinforcing the sounds of all the others. The Royal Hall's not merely a concert hall, it's a musician's way of life. Never a bad note in there, never a player wasn't energised by the tumultuous reverberation that must send back each chord singing to the man who helped create it. And, by God, Faugeras had 'em all together, all tight, neat, precise, one single instrument on which Otto Flughafer could play the Beethoven any way he wanted.

What can you do with a case like this? Some crank sends a letter and there are a million reasons why. But there are a million more letters than there are incidents. Any concert hall has a stack of them, but when was the last time anyone was injured in a concert hall?

Some of the people who send anonymous letters have a sincere desire to help, but they can't face the consequences of "interfering." Many a man sees a colleague helping himself from the till, a married man taking out a bird, a public servant accepting bribes, and he does his duty the way he sees it by sending an anonymous note. "Have you checked your till recently?" "Do you know where your husband was last night?" signed A Friend. "Ask Councillor Bates why the Housing Committee gave the building contract to his brother-in-law," signed Irate Taxpayer. . . . But some people can't live with sticking a finger into as many pies as they can find.

The wind passage I liked so much, the gentle far away melody. Effortless. Faultless. I'd planned to bring Susan to a concert, open her mind to this magic world. Clarinets growling low register in the background, chording with the rasping *cor anglais*. . . . Sarah liked Tchaikovsky and

Grieg, but drew the line at Brahms and Beethoven. Anyway, with the kids . . . and me on evening duty so often . . . I could see Faugeras eyeing Otto Flughafer with more than the usual attention. Attention tinged with a visible respect. Possibly could try Susan out on something light, a piano concerto maybe? Faugeras looked along the front desk of violins, and several players watching him smiled, as if to say, we're with you.

I glanced round the audience. They were enthralled. Not a cough or shuffle, not a move anywhere. Eyes glistened, and it felt as if the entire audience was holding its breath.

Trombones culled from some deep silence by a movement of Otto Flughafer's hand and arm, drawn and extended and held, then dismissed by a flick of his wrist that bore a mature authority. Yes, a piano concerto, that would be the best thing to try.

The manager was whispering beside me. His breath smelled of violet cachous. "Ought we to be *doing* something? Is that why they sent an *inspector?* Do you have information about it?"

"About what?" I whispered, annoyed by his interruption.

"The anonymous letter . . ." he said. "Perhaps we should stop the concert and search the Hall?"

The timpani, answered by a long glissando from the entire string section, and the woodwinds, working a delicate lace of sound tracery as a setting for this . . . *take it slow and wait for it, Flughafer's commanding hand insisted* . . . joyous chord from the brass, quite majestic.

I cursed myself for having announced my rank to Barrett. He'd read between the lines, knowing I was an inspector, and his two and two made five.

"You haven't heard something you're not telling me about?" he asked, a worried man. "It's *my* responsibility, you know. Perhaps I ought to stop the concert, so that you can bring your men and search the Hall."

"Let me look round the auditorium quietly for a while."

I suppose I would have left it at that. I would have treated myself to an hour at the concert, listening to some of the most remarkable playing I'd ever heard, my mind working beneath the surface at my problems. I was in danger of losing my job, and, in preventing drug addiction in the young girl Susan, I'd allowed her to become hooked on me, dependent on my wishes and my authority. Can it have taken only a month? She didn't smoke reefers or sell them. She didn't sleep with medical students. She didn't ride free on buses, steal from supermarkets either.

But then the phone calls began to come more frequently. Every time anyone looked at her in an interested way, she'd rush to the phone and call me. And, dammit, it seemed to happen most frequently just after I'd gone to bed. Always at home, never at the office.

Sarah chided me for trying to do too much, trying to be too much. "She needs to learn to stand on her own two feet," she said. At first we discussed Susan quite freely. I told Sarah everything, every little thing, and sought her advice. But then, one night, when I couldn't bear the thought of that oil-stinking Wimpy Bar, I took Susan to Pemberton's flat, knowing he was on duty. He'd given me his spare key when I was coming off shift, so that I could collect a tape recorder he'd got cheap but legal for my boy. I took Susan with me, to talk to her there, instead of in the Wimpy Bar. Nothing happened between us that night, but I didn't tell Sarah where we'd been and that single act of concealment seemed to destroy the trust we'd shared. Gradually, I stopped telling her about Susan, and Susan's problems. Dammit, Sarah was running my home for me, coping with everything that happened. If anything went wrong with the immersion heater, or the toaster, if one of the kids fell and grazed a leg, if the roof started to leak, Sarah had to *cope*, because I could never be relied upon to finish a job even if

I'd been able to start it. How many times had I been called out, in the old days, with the S-bend out of the kitchen sink and my tools spread everywhere. Sarah had realised I have no talent as a handy man; she didn't blame me, she simply stopped asking me to fix things and got on with them herself. And I'd come home late off duty and find her wrestling with the wringer of the washing machine that kept on packing up, and I'd swear blue bloody murder and promise faithfully to buy her a new model at the end of the month. But somehow, the money was never there to do it, or something else had cropped up that needed anything I had left over after I'd paid the bills. And Sarah learned to cope.

I went on seeing Susan whenever she needed me. You can't just abandon people.

"It's never occurred to you, I suppose," Sarah eventually said, "that you like being with that girl. From what you've told me, she's a pretty little thing . . ." And still, like a mug, I didn't see what she was getting at.

"I only hope our Helen grows up as lovely," I said, twisting the knife without knowing it.

Tears had come into Sarah's eyes, but she rubbed them angrily away and blamed the steam in the kitchen. I'd promised her an extractor fan, but hadn't got around to buying one.

"If you're not careful," she said, "that girl will become nothing but a slave to you."

"Oh, come off it. I don't need a slave . . ."

"One of these days, mark my words, you'll wake up and find you've got one. And a slave can be a big responsibility."

It was only last night she'd said that. Last night? I'd promised to paint the kitchen ceiling so that she could get on with the walls. She'd cleared as much of the furniture as she could, had covered the rest with sheets. Sarah has no head for the top of a ladder. She'd bought the emulsion, even got me a new brush out of the housekeeping. Then the phone went. It was the manager of a restaurant on Dean Street. "A young lady here says she can't pay her bill, and gave me your telephone number." I'd had to drop the painting to go and bail her out.

"I told him I'd pay him when I got my wages," Susan said. "He should have trusted me. How many times have you told me, you've got to trust people."

I suppose I would have come to a decision, sitting there in the Royal Hall, listening to that music. If Susan needed anyone, she needed people her own age, not me. Okay, so maybe she'd smoke a couple of reefers, and maybe a lad or two would take her to bed. Perhaps she'd get picked up for shoplifting and taught a sharp lesson in the magistrate's court. But I would have seen that was all part of a normal development. I'd have left the Royal Hall determined to go home and tell Sarah she could stop worrying, that this "affair" with Susan was all over. Because, let's face it, it had been an affair. Not a sexual one, not the usual furtive, greedy, my-wife-doesn't-understand-me type of affair. But I'd been flattered by Susan's youth and beauty. For a while I'd played God. Somebody had believed everything I'd said, had made me promises and kept them, had been ruled by me. And that situation was as dangerous to me as it was to her.

I suppose I'd have worked out my job problems, too. Am I any good as a copper? Wouldn't I be better off as a factory security guard, with a regular way of working. I could be some use to Sarah about the home; we could have a normal, sane, healthy, placid life. I wasn't a very good copper. I knew all the jargon, could recite the procedures backwards, but somehow I always seemed to become involved. The chief was right about that. Any case I was on was always more complicated than anybody else's cases. Take Pemberton. He can wrap up a murder fast as can be, knows his patch, put a finger on the source of almost any crime. Then to one, this robbery at Matlock's factory would be a very simple affair. I'd be running it, nominally, since I had seniority, but Pemberton would mastermind it, and it'd be a smooth operation.

All this would have become clear to me, sitting listening to that beautiful music, but suddenly, in the front tier of the second block of the stalls, I saw a man whose face was vaguely familiar. I'd checked with Barrett of course that no celebrities were in the Hall. We'd have been notified in the station of royalty or visiting foreign heads of state, and would have taken extra security precautions. Looking idly round the Hall I could spot one or two faces I knew. A conductor. A head of a television department. A couple of well-known business tycoons. That man's face was familiar but I couldn't immediately put a name to it and that niggled me. After Maurice Brigham. Faces and names are a detective's stock in trade. Jimmy Wolfingham was sitting in a box on the other side of the Hall and a young bird was looking adoringly at him. Jimmy the Con. He'd no doubt talked his way into the girl's bed as easily as he'd taken that five thousand dollars off that Canadian two years ago. No doubt who'd bought his ticket. I'd already made a mental note that Jimmy the Con was out again, but that, like I said, is part of a detective's stock in trade. That man . . . I knew I knew him. But I couldn't pin a name on him. Jack Wise. G.B.H., in the stalls almost directly below me. What's a G.B.H., grievous bodily harm, doing in a classical concert? He should be living it up in the bar of some singing pub. But then I saw the mouse next to him. Jack's brought his missus out. Mental note, Jack Wise's missus likes the classics. Never know when that nugget of knowledge might come in handy. But, that man . . .

I knew I knew that man, with that face, but I couldn't immediately say when or where or why I had known him.

Simple as that. I knew him, but who was he? Another Maurice Brigham? *His* face had been vaguely familiar, but I had failed to put a name to it.

This man was wearing a dark lounge suit. No waistcoat. A dark tie. Conventional, but not too affluent. A white shirt. That's unusual these days, implies he's square. Or has his own set of values. One hand against the far side of his cheek, his elbow on the shared arm. Some men are too timid to occupy the arms of chairs. Not much hair up front, a lot at the back, giving his head a breadth rather than height. Clean shaven, and not wearing spectacles. Not much else to see, but the general impression is on the lower side of two thousand a year. A clerk, perhaps? A shop manager? Slowly my mind catalogued each characteristic, open to impressions, hoping some little clue would reveal a feature by which I'd identify him. I KNEW I knew him, but from where? The first thing to suppose on such an occasion is that the man at whom you're looking is one of "yours." You can make mistakes that way; "one of yours" can turn out to be a respectable contact you've made off duty—someone you could embarrass if you identify them in public when you're on duty. Or, as I knew to my cost, he could turn out to be an M.P.

Who the devil was he? We're supposed to be able to recognise faces and put a name to them; mostly we can. It's part of the routine of our everyday life. This man is a suspect, bring him in for questioning. But first you have to recognise him among the fifty thousand people in a football stadium, or the thousands who walk the High Street on a Saturday morning. Faces and names, faces and identities. A face without a name is a pot without a bottom. My mind should have clicked when I saw the man I'd known briefly as Freeman. A quiet bell ought to have rung somewhere and I should have made it my business to find out more about him before involving him in that raid. It was not a name or a face I was likely to forget again.

Who was the man sitting in the auditorium? A face in the crowd, no more, no less. Dammit, I knew I had seen that face before, I damned well knew it.

Not one of mine. I'd never sent him down. He looked a bit like Harry the crooked bookie, a bit like Austin Prentiss, the con man, a bit like Arthur Swinson, assault with a deadly weapon, Tim Fairley, breaking and entering . . . Who the hell was he?

The manager leaned forward. Anxiety's contagious and you can't hide it. "Have you seen something?" he whispered.

I would have known that man's name if he'd been one of mine, so he wasn't one of mine. But who the hell was he?

"No, no one special," I said. The manager didn't believe me.

Fact number one. An anonymous note has been received. Fact number two. Most anonymous notes have no follow-up. Statistics show . . . But if ninety-nine out of a hundred anonymous notes result in no action, you might also say that one of them does. Was this the one? Fact number three. No: a supposition, not a fact. If the note meant anything, then presumably a human was involved. Presumably, something was going to happen in that Hall to cause the death of some individual, and a human would be in the Hall, either to cause it to happen, or to observe it happening.

Susan always called me "the Watcher." She said that, wherever I was, my eyes flicked backwards and forwards over the crowd. She said I never relaxed completely, never looked at her without my eyes flicking away. Looking. Always looking. I'm human too, and sometimes looking at her could bring tempting thoughts crowding to my mind. Thoughts I had no right to accept. Fact number four. I knew this man sitting in the Hall. Anonymous people, in crowds. Faces passing. Does your mind cut them out? Or are you afraid to let them in, as I was afraid sometimes to let Susan in? Because I love my wife, my kids, my life with them. Fact number five. I couldn't remember this man's name, if ever I knew it. Who was he? Man on the bus? My life had few regular patterns. I had no "Man on the 8:40, something in advertising."

Fact number six. I ought to question at least one of those students. Now is that a fact or isn't it? One school of thought would think me sloppy for not doing so immediately I had news of the anonymous note. After all, they had mounted a demonstration. I ought presumably to go to them and say, now come on, a lark's a lark, but anonymous notes are something different. But who would I question? How would I find him? Imagine it, a party of students hell bent on mischief. Suddenly the fuzz appears, breathing heavy. What happens? Either the kids are provoked into going further than they meant to, or they clear off. Fifty-fifty chance. Had I the right to take that chance, in the crowded Hall? The note had talked about a death. Could that merely be a jokey phrase implying the "death" of Beethoven's music because of the lousy way it would be played . . . ? Hardly likely. How on earth would I go about the interrogation, anyway? I'd need to get all the students out of the Hall, talk with them one by one, and that would take hours. I could hardly pop my head round the door of the Gods and say, "Hello, chaps, any of you sent an anonymous note . . . ?" It'd be no good talking to Simpson; ten to one he knew nothing about the anonymous note. No, a hundred to one. It didn't smell right, that thought that perhaps the note was a follow-up to the students' demonstration.

That man sitting in the Hall, that didn't smell right either. I let my eyes wander along the rows but each time they came back to that man. Round face, balding in front, no spectacles. Who is he? Why do I know him?

I got out of my seat and left the box. Barrett followed

me. I'd seen a telephone down the corridor in one of those acoustic alcovers. The telephone call was a hard one to make.

The desk sergeant put me straight through to the chief inspector. "I thought I told you to get lost," the chief said. "When they told me you'd gone to the Royal Hall it was almost as if the sun had started to shine again."

"An anonymous note, Chief . . ."

"The sergeant told me. Not difficult to work out who sent it . . ."

"The student demonstrators . . . ?"

"Brilliant deduction."

Two plus two equals four, eh? The chief ought to have known better than that. In police work, two plus two *never* equals four.

"There's a man here, Chief."

"Please don't hit him."

"I know him."

"You know Maurice Brigham now, but I wouldn't ask him for a reference. Who is this one?"

"That's the awkward part about it, Chief. I know I know him, but I can't put a name to him."

He laughed. "All right, I'll buy it. It has to be a gag. You're in the Royal Hall with a man whose name you don't know . . ."

"And four thousand other people . . ."

"Four thousand. That's about the same number as the messages I have for you. That breaking and entering in Chalfont Mews, for instance. They've turned up some of the silver in an antique shop in Tunbridge Wells. I want you to take the owner down to identify it. That fifteen-year-old kid, what's his name, Rogers, wants to talk to you. I think he wants to cough, but he won't cough to anybody here. The report is in from forensic about that knife you took off Corrigan. They've identified the blood group. It's the same as yours."

No case is ever neatly packaged in one go, it's like a rubber ball that goes on, bouncing and bouncing. . . .

"I've just thought of something, Chief. That stolen car job in Marlborough Mews. Only one lad can soup up an engine like that on our patch. Ted Sofflani. His place ought to be turned over."

"Now you're acting like a policeman again. Why don't you take three men and turn it over, Inspector Armstrong. And then you can come back and listen to Rogers cough, and check the forensic report on Corrigan's knife and . . ."

"I wouldn't like to leave this one, Chief. Not just yet . . ."

"Ah yes, this nameless man you *think* you know."

Ninety percent of detective work is based on good administration, but you need the other ten per cent, the intuition. I'd known the kid Rogers would cough to me. I'd spent a lot of time working him up to trust me. An incidents officer sees the cards being made out, indexed and cross-indexed, and one of them suddenly feels wrong. Now that I was thinking that way, of course Sofflani was bent. Kid in a garage, brilliant with cars, had even built himself a racer he took down to Brands Hatch. But where did he get the money? Not from selling insurance. He was bent, working on stolen cars. You pull in a man with what seems a watertight alibi, but he smells of guilt. You walk into a café or a bar, and one man, one man, sticks out a mile. I'd known that croupier was bent long before Mary told me. Who fences his stuff in Tunbridge Wells. Silver Sam. And what was Silver Sam's *modus?* Chat up the charlady, or the *au pair*. The French bit in that house in Chalfont Mews. Ten to one she'd be wearing a new coat when I went to pick her up.

This man, in the Royal Hall. I know you, you bugger.

We pay P.R.O.s to say police work is routine, diligence, and a correct observance of the Book of Rules. Any copper worth his badge will tell you the ability to smell a situation decides if you're successful or not. That man sitting quietly in the auditorium of the Royal Hall smelled wrong to me. I described him to the chief inspector. Give him credit, he thought about the description. Beneath all the banter, and despite the burdens of running a detective squad that contains individuals as difficult as me, he's still a copper.

"Doesn't mean a thing to me," he said. "What, if anything, does this man have to do with the anonymous note? That's a simple matter, Armstrong, but then I'm a simple man. I like to see connections made. So, make me a connection between this man and that note . . ."

"I can't, Chief . . ."

"Look. The students demonstrated. That's their right, and we exist, among other reasons, to preserve that right for them. But they tried to lend their activities a certain spurious drama by leaving a note on the manager's desk. It's a moot point at law whether they committed an offence or not, but we'll go into that later. Now you've seen a man. So tell me, what has this man to do with the note?"

"I don't know, Chief . . ."

"Okay, let's try something else. Why are you ringing me? It can't be for the pleasure of the sound of my voice . . ."

"I'd like three men, Chief, over here as soon as possible."

I thought he was going to explode.

"Dammit, Armstrong, every time you get your teeth into something simple, you manage to blow it up out of proportion. Three men, at this time of night, when the entire division's jumping . . . ?"

"You were prepared to give me men to turn over Sofflani's place, on nothing more than my suspicion."

"That's different. That makes sense. If you'd been thinking about it before, instead of wasting your time in the Royal Hall . . ."

"You sent me here, Chief . . ."

"I told you to get lost, and here I am talking to you on the telephone . . ."

"I know this man, Chief. Believe me, something is wrong about him."

"I know *you,* Armstrong, and I *daren't* believe you. Ten to one it's the president of the Royal College of Music."

"No, Chief, this is a wrong un, I guarantee it . . ."

"Then bring him out, and ask him what his name is. But please, please, do it gently. Don't thump him, not even by accident."

He was right, of course. Walk down the aisle, tap the man on the shoulder. Would you excuse me, sir, could I have a few words . . . ?

"I'd rather not do that, Chief."

"Because you're not sure?"

"I can't explain. It's just a feeling."

"Good God, man. A feeling, about a man you think you recognise? And all because of an anonymous note we're pretty damned certain was put there by a bunch of layabout students. And you want me to spare three men? Talk sense, Armstrong. Tell me, for example, what you thnk I should do about this kid Rogers . . ."

"He'll still be there tomorrow, Chief . . ."

"But your unidentified man won't be, eh? If you want something to do, get hold of that student chap, Simpson. You'll find out who sent that note, if you talk hard enough. And by that time the concert will be over, and you can come back here and start working on crime again. Inspector Jacobs thinks it would be worth while talking to that Murphy woman. He thinks she's the one who's running the shoplifting gang. Or don't you want me to remind you that's another of your unsolved cases?"

He didn't need to rub it in. Everybody thinks we solve all our cases. Too many damned television programmes where the crime is exposed, solved, and wrapped up between the shampoo and the toothpaste. I was working on at least fifteen separate cases, all simultaneously. Damn it, my days were like a patchwork quilt. Start off with an investigation of a statement in a hold-up, interrogate a junkie, look at a stolen car, talk to a woman about a man allegedly seen exposing himself, see a witness about the death by stabbing of a prostitute, file my crime returns, remember to get a present for Helen's birthday, eat lunch—that's a joke, more likely grab a sandwich—talk to Susan, ring Sarah to tell her I'd be late. . . .

Give the chief credit. He put down the telephone gently. But the click was just as final as if he'd slammed it.

Quickly I dialled my home number. I'd just remembered. I'd promised to call Sarah to tell her what time I'd be home. She was making steak and kidney pie, and needed to know to within half an hour.

The number was engaged. Dammit, Helen on the line most probably. Talking to that chum of hers. Kids! They spend all day together at school and then waste a fortune and half the evening talking to each other on the telephone.

Susan had told me that was why she didn't ring me earlier. Because when she tried, the phone was often engaged. I'd have to do something about Susan. Obviously it couldn't go on the way it was. Sarah was right. It was getting to a stage where I'd have to choose between my wife and kids and Susan. Dammit, she was as demanding as if I was her steady. In a way I was her steady. She hadn't made any girl friends at the hostel. And all the boys wanted to take her to bed. Couldn't blame them. She had a ripe luscious figure, rich full breasts. Sarah was a bit short in that department. I didn't mind, but she could have done with a bit more. Like Susan had . . . Dammit, I thought, I do fancy the girl.

CHAPTER 3

I went back to the box. Barrett was hovering by the door. "Just checking in," I said, but I don't think he believed me. We went into the box together and sat down. I was looking at the orchestra, deliberately not at the man in the auditorium. Barrett was watching me. If he'd been a nail-biter, they'd have been down to the quick. Slowly I let my gaze roam back across the heads of the audience, until the man was again in my vision. Still I didn't know his name.

"Who do *you* think sent the note?" I asked Barrett.

"I *did* think the students. I thought it was all part of that silly childish demonstration they put on . . ."

"But now you're not so sure . . ."

"You've made me worried."

"Why? Because I'm an inspector? Because I appear to be taking this note seriously? It's my job to treat every inquiry as a serious one."

"Not that exactly. It's something, well, in the atmosphere, you might say." Good for you, Barrett, you can smell it too.

"Could you find that chap Simpson for me? Easily and quickly?"

Barrett thought for a moment. "He's up in the Gods. We don't have numbered seats. He could be anywhere. It's not very light and there'll be a lot of people, all packed in together. It would be very hard to get to him, even if I knew what he looked like . . ."

"You don't know what he looks like?"

"I have never met him. Everything has been done by correspondence. He wrote to me as the secretary of the Music Society, I replied as the manager of the Royal Hall."

Yes, it would be like that, wouldn't it? "You'll have to put it in writing." Try not to meet people since, once you've met them, you become involved with them. They can say, "Oh, Barrett, I've met him," and perhaps that gives them a leverage. Avoid face to face encounter, and you avoid people ringing up and saying, "Mr. Barrett, you remember me? We met at XYZ. I wondered if I might ask a favour of you . . . ?"

"We talked on the telephone, of course, but I've no idea what he looks like. Does it matter?"

"If you had been able to identify him, I could have had a few words with him and perhaps we'd have got to the bottom of this thing very quickly."

He was silent for a few moments, thinking, his owlish eyes opening and shutting as if to energise his thoughts. He was completely out of his depth. No yardstick with which he could judge this situation. I felt sorry for him. We're used to launching ourselves into the unknown. We leave the station, never knowing where we'll wind up, what time we'll be back. He couldn't survive a single day of such a life. "So," he said, "you think there's something in this anonymous note . . . ?"

"I didn't say that."

"Then why do you want to talk to Simpson?" He was clutching at familiar patterns. You talk to people only when something goes wrong. So, if you want to talk to someone, something must be wrong. "I'd better call the chairman of the board of governors," he said. "I'd better stop the concert."

I had to avoid the possibility of him taking the bit between his teeth and galloping off scared. As manager he had his rights and his duties. He *could* stop the concert without reference to me, but that was the last thing I wanted. I felt in my bones that the concert must be allowed to proceed normally.

"Simpson knew about the demonstration. He might know something about the letter."

"Do *you* think I ought to stop the concert?" he asked.

"No, I don't."

"I ought to ring the chairman."

"No, I wouldn't do that. Not yet. No point in worrying him unduly. Not yet, anyway." No matter what the chief may say about my clumsiness, about the way things often seem to go wrong when I'm in charge, he can't deny I can handle people, in my own way. I'd handled that boy Rogers, hadn't I, so that now he was ready to tell me everything I wanted to know. I could handle Barrett, given time. "After all, you don't want to ring him about nothing, do you, make yourself look a worrier . . ."

Right on the button. He cared what the chairman thought about him. Wouldn't want to expose his weakness to the board. And he was a worrier, I was sure of that.

"Perhaps you're right," he said.

Four thousand people in that concert hall, an orchestra, a choir of a hundred people sitting behind the orchestra. In this work the choir doesn't perform until the last movement. Four soloists sitting near the front of the orchestra. Looking animated with professional ease.

"You'll have a death on your hands," the note said. But whose death? Choir, orchestra, soloist, conductor? Member of the audience? Even a member of the staff? I looked at Barrett. "How many staff on duty?"

"What kind of staff?"

"All kinds."

"Twenty-five . . ."

"Twenty-six including yourself . . . ?" I had a sudden thought. If I was right about this man, possibly someone on his staff might be gunning for him. Or someone recently fired.

"Anyone ever threatened you, Mr. Barrett?" I asked. "You personally." I kept my voice deliberately calm and for a second he didn't catch the implication. "Of course not," he said, "why should they?"

"Anyone ever threatened you on behalf of—I mean as the representative of—the Hall?"

"The *Royal* Hall," he said automatically.

"Have you had occasion to discharge anyone recently?"

He shook his head. "No, I can't think why anyone should threaten me, either personally or on behalf of the Hall. And I haven't had occasion to discharge anyone for, oh, nearly a year."

It was slow getting to him, but then I saw his face flush. He got up and left the box. I followed him.

"Do you think they're after *me?*" he asked.

"I haven't said they're after *anybody.*"

"But you asked if anyone has threatened me . . ."

"Just routine. Like that business of finding the man Simpson, trying to suggest a possible short cut."

"I really must ring the chairman," he said. Let him ring the chairman, and the chairman would be on to the chief inspector and I'd have fire and brimstone dripping down my neck. "A death on your hands, that's what the note said. Because I'm merely doing my job?"

Killing takes hate. Barrett was smug, distant, unapproachable, petty, unsympathetic, but no one could hate him enough to want to kill him.

"The first sign of anything I find wrong," I said crisply, "you can call the chairman. Until then, I'd rather you didn't." Crisp, cool, calm, collected. A police inspector, with a known authority. That was something he could understand.

"Shall we clear the Hall, Inspector?" Barrett said.

"What good would that do?"

"Then you search it."

"Looking for what?"

"If somebody is intending to kill somebody, he might have a weapon under one of the seats?"

"And use it while we're clearing the Hall." He hadn't thought of that. What did the anonymous note mean? Assuming it to be serious, not just a student's joke. AT THE END OF THE CHORAL SYMPHONY, YOU'LL HAVE A DEATH ON YOUR HANDS. So, during the Choral Symphony, the work the orchestra was performing so brilliantly, somebody would die. Or be killed. Or kill themselves.

How? Well, how many ways are there of killing yourself, or killing somebody else? Poison, a knife, a gun. We could rule out assault with a blunt and deadly weapon since the killing would need to be certain. Poison would be difficult. Would it? No, when you came right down to it. Crowds milling around, poison in the end of a needle or a dart, and it's the easiest thing in the world to scrape somebody with a needle or a dart in a crowd. Easier than shooting a gun, or throwing a knife. A dart perhaps? Need to have an extraordinary good aim to use a dart. Imagine going for double top, just under somebody's ear. In a crowd. A bow and arrow. Sounds fanciful, but then killing's a fanciful matter. They keep a skull at the Police College. Just to confound young recruits. The skull has a hole in it the size of a fifty pence piece; ask any recruit and he'll say the cause of death was assault with a deadly weapon, or a blunt instrument. He'd be wrong. A little old man bored of life locked himself into a greenhouse and tapped away at his own head with a coal hammer. Despite the hole he broke into his skull, what must have been intense pain, and the blood running down the side of his head, he didn't die. He can't even have lost consciousness because eventually, realising the coal hammer method was no good, he cut his throat to finish himself. You can't get more fanciful about death than that.

Bow and arrow. An acceptable murder weapon. The person using it would need to be a good shot, but anybody who goes in for archery would need to be a good shot when you think of the size of the target they put the arrows in and the long range. Robin Hood's exploits are a damned sight more credible than Wyatt Earp's. Range of twenty yards. The archer could be sitting in a box, just as I had been, hiding behind the curtains with which the boxes were draped. Or standing up somewhere, behind a curtain. Anywhere where nobody could see him to watch what he was doing. Draw a bead, whang an arrow into anyone in that auditorium, or on the platform. Then drop the bow, walk into the nearest lavatory, and we'd never pin it on him. Arrow, gun, knife, which could it be? Commandos could throw a six-inch nail and get double top every time. Russians fire cyanide bullets like needles; that's how they got that man in Munich. Needles. A hypodermic needle jabbed through the back of the seat. Victim feels a momentary discomfort, no more, thinks the fabric is a bit sharp, or the seat has a loose spring, possibly even starts to put his hand behind him when the poison hits. Man behind escapes in the hubbub caused by his victim's collapse.

That man whose face I recognised, whose name I couldn't remember. He was still sitting there. And he still smelled of something. So did that anonymous note. Damn it, that note wasn't a student prank. Despite everything, despite Maurice Brigham, my divided loyalties between Sarah and Susan, an overfilled personal dossier, and the chief's specific instructions to get lost, I rang him again. They should have given me the medal for bravery.

"Glad you rang, Armstrong," he said. "I'm giving you a stake-out. Tuesday night . . ."

"I was ringing about that note, Chief . . ."

"All the details in your in tray," he said, as if I hadn't spoken, as if the note had never been received.

"Mattox Factory?"

"That's right. Pemberton's had a whisper. Gang of six."

"I've heard some of Pemberton's whispers."

"Reliable informant, Armstrong. Not like some of yours." Ouch, that hurt. A policeman depends on his informants; good or bad you have to take a chance. Of late, mine had been bad.

"About this note, Chief . . ."

"You've found who wrote it, eh?"

"No, Chief, I haven't."

"You've located that student fellow, Simpson?"

"No, Chief, not yet."

"Not achieving very much, are you, Armstrong?"

"That man's still here . . ."

"Not likely to walk out in the middle of the concert, is he? What about the manager, Barrett?"

"How do you mean, what about him, Chief?"

"What does he think?"

"He's waiting for me to tell him what to do."

"We're all waiting for you to tell us what to do, Inspector Armstrong."

"I know this man, Chief, I'm convinced I know him."

"I don't doubt that. I'll go along with that. But who is he? By the way, what's your telephone number there?" I gave him the number of the box. Then he made me describe Nameless again. The description meant nothing to him.

"What does the note look like?"

"Ballpoint pen on a page from a pad. Probably Ryman's."

"Any prints?"

"I want to have it tested, in a hurry."

"Any distinguishing features? Perfume on the paper, special marks, you know what to look for?"

"Yes, Chief, and I know how to waste a lot of time finding it." He didn't like that. Dumb insolence. Sometimes it's the only weapon you have. But an anonymous note investigation at the scientific level can take weeks. A few whiffs of perfume. The forensic labs can take weeks identifying it as Ma Rêve which can be bought over the counter of every supermarket. A drop of oil on the corner of an envelope and days later they tell you the note has been handled by someone who, at some time or other, has been inside a Shell garage. . . .

My only hope, and it was a slender one, would be to find a fingerprint. It's one thing to be acutely conscious of something wrong, to sit with all your nerve ends twitching, and another to be able to convince a senior police officer of the need to take men away from the investigation of actual crime. I know how understaffed we are. A policeman never has an idle moment; there never is a time when you can find a spare copper, either uniformed or detective. My days always started the same way, which of the one hundred things I've got to do today will I do first, and always ended with, which of them have I not done.

The time was now 2015. Only fifty-seven minutes of music left. AT THE END OF THE CHORAL SYMPHONY, YOU'LL HAVE A DEATH ON YOUR HANDS.

"I need those three men, Chief, over here, in a hurry."

"All right," the chief inspector said, "since you're so insistent you can have three men." There was vinegar on his mucous membrane. "But I want a complete search made, and if there is anyone or anything, I want him or it found. And I want to be kept informed of progress."

I could almost hear his mind flicking over the pages of procedure in the Rule Book. What to do in the event of . . . a threatening letter in a public place. First, search the public place and attempt to find, and then to disarm or remove, any offensive weapon of any kind, calling in such external services as may be necessary. That was a face-saving way of saying if it's a bomb, don't muck about with it but call in the Army. Then he'd turn to the page marked "Delegation of Responsibility": "Any Officer to whom responsibility for an Inquiry has been delegated by a Senior Officer becomes responsible for the outcome of any action he may take." A nice way of saying, if you make a balls-up of anything it's your own head that goes on the chopping block.

"And I'm holding you fully responsible, Inspector," he said. He put down the telephone. There were a number of clicks on the line and the desk sergeant cut in. The chief had pressed what we call the "Get to Hell" button, and I was on my own, adrift on a page of neatly delineated responsibilities.

"Inspector Armstrong?"

"Yes, Sergeant . . . I want . . ."

"There's been a young girl here looking for you . . ."

"Later, Sergeant. I want . . ."

"She seems very bothered, Inspector. Said it was a vital she should talk to you, right away. She left a message."

The sergeant was a methodical man. Everything in its proper order. Everything "chronological," that was his phrase.

"Right, Sergeant, give me the message but hurry it up."

"Right, Inspector. Got your pencil ready . . ."

"Hurry it up . . ."

"Right, Inspector. The message says, Must see you. Going back to hostel, well, it could be either hostel, Inspector, or hotel."

"It's hostel, Sergeant . . ." I knew it would be Susan.

"Oh, know her, do we . . . ?"

"Yes. But forget about the message for a moment. . . ." It would be Susan, and another of her problems that she could solve for herself if only she'd grow up. At that moment I was in no mood to consider the problems of a love-sick young kid I ought not to be messing about with anyway. I gave the sergeant my instructions. Told him which box I was in. Heard him bellow the orders that would get three men speedily on the way. When I hung up the phone, Barrett was standing by my elbow. A very worried man. He'd heard me ask for help. The note hadn't troubled him except as an administrative inconvenience. Too many people too often had cried "Wolf" for him to be bothered by yet another note. We have a cupboardful back at the station. When the police, in its majesty, had seen fit, or so he thought, to give the note the importance of an investigating inspector rather than the more usual constable, he had started to wonder if perhaps there might be something in it. The lives and safety of four thousand people were in his hands but that would have been nothing to him compared with the thought that perhaps he himself was about to be knocked off. When I called for help, he really panicked.

"I'm going to clear the Hall," he said.

I grabbed his arm. "You'll do no such thing until I authorise it."

"It's my responsibility."

"No, it's not," I said. "You've asked the police to undertake an investigation and that's exactly what I am doing."

"You can't stop me. I'm manager here," he blustered.

I was still gripping his arm. "At your request I am undertaking an investigation," I said slowly. "You must know it is an offence to impede the police in the course of their inquiries. An offence."

Assume we have a suspect, by accepting the note is genuine. That's the first step. Start back from that point. A guilty suspect. That was one of my first lessons from an old hand who forgot it only once and wound up with a knife in his belly in the days of the Brighton race gangs. So, start off by assuming that Nameless out there, whoever he may be, was guilty. Of what? Of sending an anonymous note? Or of taking steps to make the contents of the note come true? Conduct whereby a breach of the peace might be occasioned?

A little man, sitting in the Royal Hall, smiling to himself at the thought he's sent an anonymous note, that within a few minutes he'll be responsible for someone's death.

Why, for God's sake? Why?

Don't ask why. Ask what. And when, and where, and how. You know when and where, don't you? In the Royal Hall, sometime during the playing of this Beethoven symphony. No time for *why; why* takes too long and sometimes you never know it. Sometimes when you do know it you can't believe it. So, all we need to find out is *what* he intends to do, and *how* he intends to do it, assuming we start with the *who* known to us, the nameless man in the Hall.

But is that a safe assumption? Damn it, he could be nothing more than a smart-ass music critic.

Assume that man out there is going to kill someone. What we must discover quickly is, how does he intend to do it? What are the possibilities? He has some kind of weapon concealed about him, and at a suitable moment he'll use it. That puts his intended victim within his range. Whoever his intended victim may be. At a symphony concert the most logical victim would be the conductor, since he's the most obvious target. But why do it at the concert, when escape is presumably more difficult? . . . He can't stand up and fire a rifle, that's certain. A pistol, maybe. With some kind of silencing device, possibly? But silencers cut distance, and that means his victim would need to be much nearer to him than the conductor is at present. You need to be a damn good pistol shot, even with an unsilenced pistol, to guarantee to hit the figure of a man at that range. A pistol would be easy to conceal, to produce and use. But once he fires the pistol he's got to get out of the Hall with it. And paraffin tests will point the finger at anyone who's recently fired a pistol, so we just block the doors and give everybody a paraffin test coming out and catch the man who did it.

Possibly he intends to get out of his seat at the appropriate time, and place himself somewhere nearer to his victim, somewhere near an exit so that he can slip out unobserved. That would be the smart thing to do. Possibly he's got a knife, and intends to use that. Possibly the AT THE END OF THE CHORAL SYMPHONY is a blind. Perhaps he intends to get out of his seat on the pretext of going to the lavatory, and hide himself behind a curtain, in a corner, anywhere he can level a pistol, take aim and fire, and still hope to get away with it in the confusion. Possibly he has a knife he means to use on someone, close-up, in the crush bar during the interval. He could get away with that more easily than if a shot had been fired. If you're right-handed you hold the knife blade upwards up your sleeve, down the side of your body. You work your way through the crowd. When you reach your victim you position yourself behind him on his left. The heart side. You let the knife drop down in your hand until the blade comes clear of your sleeve. The knife points upwards. You start to walk past your victim on his left, and your right arm trails behind you. It's a perfectly natural movement. As you draw level with your victim you lift your arm and jab the point and as much of the blade of the knife as you can get up into his heart from the back and the side. You leave the knife in there, make a left turn, and you can be two yards away before your victim starts to fall, before anyone can see the knife sticking out of his back. It takes a professional. Or a hating man, a nut.

That's when another thought struck me: I had assumed he meant to get away with it, but was that necessarily so? A nut may not care whether he lives or dies. In that case, the offensive weapon could easily be a bomb, or an incendiary.

Still I worried. Why send a note? Why? But I thrust the thought from me. *Why* must come later, not now, not yet.

The three men arrived, checking box numbers until they saw me waiting impatiently. Skelton, Cooper, and Sergeant Bates. Three coppers without a drop of intuition among them. Cooper didn't like me; his expense vouchers were often a work of fiction, and though I don't mind a bit of fiddling he was downright venal. Skelton was a good lad who'd make sergeant one day, if he could learn the regulations. Sergeant Bates would never make inspector; he didn't have the admittedly small amount of brain power needed. Three coppers with eyes, ears, hands, but no "nose."

"I hear we've got to do a search," Sergeant Bates said by way of greeting. "Three of us isn't enough to search this place . . ."

"You don't need to tell me that, Sergeant Bates. I'm going to concentrate all our efforts on one man. Let me give you the background before you make up your mind what can and can't be done. An anonymous note has been received. It says, 'At the end of the Choral Symphony,' and that is what they're now playing, 'you'll have a death on your hands.' Sergeant Bates, you take the note. Do what you like with it, and I'll bear the responsibility, but within fifteen minutes I want an identification of any fingerprints you can find on it."

"It can't be done," Sergeant Bates said but, give him credit, he was already moving away.

"Cooper?"

"Yes, Inspector."

"That man, first row of second section, four seats from the centre aisle on the right-hand side. Describe him."

He did, whispering the words standing in the back of the box where nobody could observe him.

"Right. Photograph that face in your mind and put a name to it within fifteen minutes, right?"

"That can't be done either," he said, echoing Sergeant Bates. But unlike the sergeant he was smiling. Then he too left the box. On his way to our library. He'd call out the description to our librarian, a sergeant with thirty-five years on the force who had the features of every known criminal fixed in his mind. He'd stand at the photograph file and start to flick 'em out for Cooper to check: full face, side shot, left and right. We have a photograph of every known criminal in our area with a description of all their nasty little activities.

"Skelton?"

"Yes?" He was a whippet straining at the lead.

"You know the man we're interested in?"

"I know where he's sitting, Inspector."

"Right. I want you within spitting distance of him. Don't take your eyes off him for one single second. He may have a knife or a pistol. He may have a bag at his feet, with a bomb in it, or an incendiary in his pocket. Damn it, he could have a bow and arrow or a poisoned blow-pipe stuck up his trouser leg. Whatever he's got I want you near enough to stop him using it. And I don't want him to see or hear you, I don't want him to know you're there. Understand?"

"Yes, Inspector."

Nameless might not wait for the ending of the symphony before he pulled whatever he intended to do, if he suspected we were closing in on him. Of course I knew what the textbook said. I knew I'd get hell from the chief inspector for doing this thing my way. The rules said I should have stopped the concert and cleared the Hall the minute I had any reasonable suspicion anything was wrong in there. Or, if I didn't stop the concert, and I had reason to suspect this nameless man, I ought to go in there, tap him on the shoulder, and ask him to come to the manager's office to answer a couple of questions. That's what the Rule Book said. Meanwhile the three men the chief so reluctantly had sent to me should have been sent to search the building. I've never done anything by the Rule Book.

One half of my mind warned me to leave my options open, not to put all my eggs in the one basket that had Nameless on it. But my experience has taught me that a plan, once made, can be switched very quickly at its focal point. Okay, so if the anonymous note meant something but had originated from some other person in the Hall, I'd have to swing the plan around. But for the moment, I was gambling on it being Nameless who eventually would make the move.

The man who sent the note could have a bomb, could be sitting anywhere in the Hall with the detonator in his hands. The second anybody walked on to that platform to stop the concert, he'd know he'd been twigged. Ten to one, no, a hundred to one, he'd start the mechanism, put down the bomb, and get out of the building fast, while the man on the platform appealed to everyone to file out slowly. In the confusion, no one would remember the man who got out in a hurry.

Nothing must happen in that auditorium to alert him. Absolutely nothing. So far as the audience was concerned, that concert must carry on normally, of that I was convinced.

Quite irrelevantly, I suddenly remembered. I had to ring Dick Allsop to tell him about the silver that had turned up in Tunbridge Wells, and I'd better ring Sarah to tell her I'd be late for her steak and kidney pie, and to say I'd forgotten to get the hockey boots Helen needed for school, and the bank manager had agreed to let us go into the red for the deposit on the educational cruise we'd agreed to let Robin take next spring. Dammit, she'd be cross about the hockey boots. Or else, more likely, she wouldn't have relied on me remembering and would have bought them herself.

Which would mean giving her extra housekeeping on Friday.

The concert manager had disappeared, and I hadn't seen him go. When he came back he was panting, but he handed me a pair of binoculars.

"Bless you," I said and took them from him. As I stood at the back of the box and held them to my eye to focus them, I spoke to him. "Now here's something else you can do for me. Put your electricians behind three spotlights. Anywhere high up at the front, but where they can't be seen from the auditorium. I want three spotlights trained on the man sitting down there, centre aisle, four seats in, first row of the second block, got him?"

"Yes, I have him. Who is he? Someone I should know?"

"It doesn't matter who he is for the moment. I want three spotlights aiming at him, but not switched on. Give your electricians the instruction that if anything happens in the Hall, anything suspicious at all, or if you or I shout 'light,' they'll switch the lights on and use 'em to dazzle that man. Is that understood?"

He stood there. I could sense that he had not moved though I was looking through the glasses. I put the glasses down.

"Please, please can we clear the Hall?" he asked.

I shook my head.

"I'll have to telephone my chairman," he said.

"Look, do me a favour. Get the lights fixed the way I want 'em. And then, you can put in a call to Beethoven himself. . . ."

Barrett to chairman. Chairman to commissioner. Commissioner to division. Division to the chief detective inspector and him to me. Chop.

Clear the Hall, that's what the good book said, that's what Barrett wanted. But I dare not do it. Assume Nameless was the one. Assume the letter was not a complete hoax, assume Nameless was the one the anonymous correspondent had warned us about. There could be no sense in alerting him now by ordering the Hall cleared.

From where I was sitting in the corner of the back of that box, with the glasses to my eyes, I could see Skelton start to move down the aisle of that second section, cautiously. To me he looked every inch a copper. To anyone in the Hall I prayed he'd look like an usher, going to offer somebody coffee during the interval. But to me, he had that set to his body that said he was there on lawful business, that out-of-the-common-rut look that says "I'm different." Slowly he moved forward, a step at a time, as if he was too polite to disturb the worshippers in some shrine.

And, incidentally, that was how the orchestra was playing and the audience was reacting, as if in some shrine, some temple of divine music.

Through the binoculars I could see the face of Nameless quite clearly, quite distinctly. Thank God they don't put out the lights at concerts, only dim them a fraction. I could see his lips moving as he followed the theme. I do that myself if I know the work, and I think I could have conducted the Beethoven Ninth. Though not like Flughafer. I could see Nameless's eyes move from section to section of the orchestra anticipating the score. Suddenly, someone must have moved because the light altered, and through the glasses I could see a dark bundle on Nameless's lap. A bundle on his lap? In a concert? An oddity. What the hell could it be? His coat? A parcel? A hold-all? It was big enough to hold a knife, a pistol, or a bomb. Would the chief inspector accept that as legitimate grounds for suspicion. "This man, Chief, I know his face but not his name, but he does have something in his lap. . . ."

He wasn't wearing a top coat, but nobody in the Hall was wearing a top coat. It wasn't that sort of night. A few people had light raincoats in their laps. Okay, so it's a black raincoat. They're very popular this year. So think. Think. Obviously the first thought says, as the chief himself had said, "Go in there and pull him out."

Think. Reasons for *not* going in there to pull him out. One. You have no idea *who* he is, but for the purposes of mounting some sort of counteraction you've assumed he is the source of the anonymous note and the source of any attempt at the life of anyone in that Hall. That is only an *assumption.* So reason says, wait until you have some more evidence before you actually *act* on that assumption, other than taking a few anticipatory measures.

Two. If that man *is* the one, and if he has a controllable device, and if you scare him, and if . . . No need to think any further on that particular issue. Whatever you do, you must not run that risk. You dare not, with the lives of all those people at stake.

Consider all the possibilities. That's how we'd been trained, how I'd trained my lads. So far I'd assumed that if death was to be caused, it would be by the projection of some lethal device, a knife or a bullet. I'd also assumed Nameless would be the point of projection. Smother the act of projection, via Skelton, and we prevent the death. Q.E.D. If we could contain Nameless when it came to the crucial moment. If Skelton could contain him. It takes a brave man to be a criminal, and many of my young lads forget that. They despise criminals and treat 'em as cowards, assuming that once apprehended they'll come quietly. But, I tell them, just study what a criminal has to do in the act of committing a crime, and you'll see that often the criminal must be a braver man than your average constable. Think of the skill and courage of a lag who'll climb a drainpipe, enter a darkened room where someone may be asleep, and walk across that room without showing a peep of light, not knowing what natural or unnatural thing is waiting for him. What does a householder do when he surprises a burglar? He grabs a poker, starts laying about him in panic. The burglar knows that, and yet finds the courage to enter and cross a room in the pitch black of night. No wonder many of them, when they're caught, fight like tigers.

Would Nameless fight like a tiger when Skelton jumped him? And in the fight, might he get out the pistol or the knife and use it? Or, worse thought still, it he's sitting with a bomb might he not press the button that fires it?

Barrett had returned. "Did you telephone the chairman?"

He shook his head. "I ought to," he said, "those are my instructions and I ought to obey them."

"If it would make you feel better, give him a ring. Tell him you've found an anonymous note, you've handed it over to the police, and they've started such action as they think fit. Tell him you've asked for the Hall to be cleared, but the police have declined. I don't mind," I said. The poor bastard had to live with himself and his board of trustees after this night was over. "Before you telephone him, however, will you do one thing more for me? See your commissionaires, or whoever is in charge of the doors, so that all the doors are locked."

James Barrett was aghast. "Lock the doors," he said. "That's in direct contravention of the County Council and fire regulations."

"I know it is, but please don't argue with me. I want every door locked, and a commissionaire standing guard on each one. And if anybody tries to go out through any one of those doors, I want him detained until I can get there."

"But what happens if there is a panic? What if anything, well, you know, happens? People always rush for the doors at moments like that."

"Give your commissionaires instructions that, if a crowd comes running, they're to unlock the doors and fling them open immediately. And stand back so they won't get crushed. . . ."

James Barrett thought about that. "I don't like it," he said, "we've never had anything like this when they've sent a constable over."

"I know you haven't." Cup of tea in the snack bar, or a bottle of beer, then a slow wander round the corridors, putting off the evil moment of going out onto the cold street again. "Don't worry, Mr. Barrett, I'll take full responsibility. I'll tell your entire board of trustees, if you like, that I used my authority as a police officer to order you to do these things . . . in writing if that'll make you move quicker . . ."

"That will not be necessary," he said as he left the box.

One or two people in the auditorium had glanced at the box in annoyance; I hadn't realised the sound of our whispering would reach that far.

Bates came back first. "You're out of luck," he said. "No prints on the note except those of Mr. Barrett."

"In luck," I said.

"How so?"

"No prints . . . ? That's unnatural. If the note was a gag who'd have bothered wiping prints off it?"

"I see what you mean."

You bet he saw what I meant. It's not easy to wipe prints off a sheet of paper: the paper must never be handled, except with gloves; must be taken from the centre of a pack or must be chemically treated to remove those thin veins of perspiration on which the print is based. Perhaps the chief would believe me now.

"You see that documentary on crime control, Inspector?" Sergeant Bates asked me. "Last week they were dealing with fingerprints. That sort of stuff shouldn't be put out on television. Almost a classroom lesson of how to beat the police . . ."

How many millions watch television every night? We'd have been lucky to find prints on that note.

Barrett returned, and sat on a chair at the back of the box. I was still using the binoculars to sweep the Hall, returning all the time to Nameless. Sergeant Bates came close to me and whispered. "You don't think we ought to clear the Hall, Inspector?" he asked.

I shook my head. Nameless had just taken something out of the bundle on his knee. It could have been a toffee. He placed it in his mouth. He put his hand back into the bundle. Damn it, the light didn't penetrate there between the rows. What was that bundle? An overcoat? A bag?

"If we start to clear the Hall, that just might trigger something, Sergeant. You can never tell in a case like this . . ."

"Assuming there is something to trigger? And someone trigger it, Inspector."

"Assuming . . ." It wasn't his responsibility, and he knew it, but he was carefully planting his alibi. "At 2018 hrs whilst standing with the inspector in a box, keeping the crowd under surveillance, I took the liberty of suggesting to the inspector, despite him being my superior officer, that it might be a good idea to clear the Hall. . . ."

Skelton moved down the Hall. Beckoned with authority to the man sitting one seat behind Nameless, one seat to the side. The man got up and came out and Skelton walked to the back of the Hall with him. Nameless showed no interest, too occupied with the music. Skelton's a good man. He found the man he'd moved a spare seat at the back of the Hall, and then he walked down the aisle again, and sat in the seat behind Nameless. It had only taken a half a minute in all, with no sign of anything unusual—just some idiot, people would think, who can't read the seat numbers on his ticket. Only the man himself would have seen the police badge, and he'd be round afterwards to ask what it was all about. We keep a few bottles of beer in the canteen for soothing ruffled feathers, and charge them to the public relations account. Or knock it off a copper's pay, if he's in the wrong.

Nameless hadn't turned around, gave no sign of noticing anything. Now the surveillance starts. How many times I'd done just that very thing, in the crowd at a football match waiting for some thief to pass the stuff to the fence, in theatres, on buses, placing myself near enough to the suspect to be able to grab him with anything he tried to pass, near enought to anticipate any sudden move he might make, and if necessary stop him making it. There was a great danger of some sort of telepathic communication taking place between watcher and watched. The technique I'd worked out and had tried to teach my lads was constantly to look away and look back, never stare, never hold a rigid gaze at anyone. Move your eyes and not your head if the suspect is looking in your direction. Eye movements can be masked, head movements are noticeably larger and the subconscious records them; the fiftieth time they happen, "that bugger's watching me," the suspect says to himself. From that moment, the watcher is on the danger list. The roles are reversed, with the watcher now being watched, often by a desperate man.

Skelton had rested his arm on the seat in front of him. He was sitting slightly hunched forward. It was a familiar posture. His weight's on his feet, not on his arse. That hand and arm could lick out with the speed of a snake, and Skelton's whole body could follow it, if necessary.

Nameless kept putting his hand in his lap, but now he didn't put his hand immediately to his lips, so it couldn't have been sweets. He seemed to put his hand into his lap to reassure himself, but he never glanced down, never took his gaze from the orchestra, never looked at any other member of the audience, as most people do from time to time in a concert hall, when the lights are on. I do it myself all the time. I look at the orchestra, watch them playing the passages I know and like, but then I look at other people in the audience, to see if they're enjoying it as much as I am, hating it like I am. Was it suspicious that Nameless never looked about him, as if he dared not, as if he might be afraid of catching the eye of someone who could recognise him? Damn it, I'd recognised him, hadn't I? I couldn't put a name to him yet, and therefore I didn't know why I recognised him. Perhaps he was in the relationship of watcher and watched, with his intended victim at the other end of it. The people in front of him and slightly to the side appeared to have nothing special about them, and certainly I'd never seen them before. A youngish couple, early thirties, possibly married, certainly not very demonstrative towards each other. Not holding hands or arms, not inclining towards each other. I wouldn't have known they were together if the woman hadn't whispered in the man's ear, and the man smiled at her. Next to them a music lover, score open on his knees, following every bar, looking up and frowning every time Otto Flughafer's conducting varied from that academic and no doubt uninspired version of the Beethoven he carried about with him. Next to him, a woman about fifty, who may have been with the woman sitting next to her or may not. They'd had no communication together while I had been watching. She was a "superior" lady, with what she hoped was a dash of quality, but no doubt smelling faintly of eau-de-cologne and cooking.

The concert manager was tugging my sleeve. Cooper was on the telephone. I gave the glasses to Sergeant Bates and went out without instructing him. Let the bastard use his own initiative.

"You're out of luck," Cooper said.

"That's the second time I've heard that in five minutes."

"There's nothing in the file. . . . The chief inspector says . . ."

"Get back here. . . ."

The bastard. So he'd been to the chief inspector, had he? The damned arse-licking creep. "Sir, sir, the inspector has asked me to . . ." Cooper knew about responsibilities all right, and wanted desperately to get a few for himself, along with the next sergeant's stripe. There's one in every station.

Since I was standing by the telephone I placed a call to Sarah. This time the number was not engaged. "You really must tell our Helen not to occupy the phone all evening," I said.

"It wasn't our Helen. It was *your* Susan."

I don't know why I was riled. Perhaps it was because she called her "my Susan." Or the hockey boots. Or the steak and kidney pie . . . "She is not *my* damned Susan," I said. "I wish for God's sake you wouldn't keep calling her that. . . ."

There was a shocked silence at the other end of the telephone. We don't talk to each other like that normally.

"I wish I didn't have to call her anything," she said. "I wish you were finished with her. I've told you over and over again, you take too much on yourself. You haven't even got time to look after your family properly, without taking on other responsibilities."

That hurt. "What do you mean, look after you properly? . . . You never go short . . ."

"Have you got the hockey boots?"

She knew I hadn't.

"Are you coming home for steak and kidney pie?"

She knew I wasn't.

"She talked to me for half an hour. I couldn't get her off the telephone." Previously, whenever Susan had rung, I'd always been there. So far as I knew, this was the first time Sarah had had an actual conversation with her.

"What did she want . . . ?"

"I don't know. She wouldn't say."

"You can't have talked for half an hour about nothing."

"I wasn't doing the talking. Frankly, I was wishing the pigs had her. The kids were waiting for their suppers . . ."

"So what did she say . . . ?"

"She didn't say anything. Not straight out. Just asked me about you. When you'd be back. Where you were likely to be, what you were likely to be doing. I told her, I make a strict rule never, never, to ring you up at work."

That was perfectly true. Sarah wasn't one to bother you when you're out of the house. What happened between my leaving and returning was strictly my affair. She was interested, of course, in anything I might care to tell her, but I was never obliged to account for my time.

"So you don't know what she wanted?"

"I think she just wanted to talk to somebody. That's a woman's thing you wouldn't know anything about. Sometimes, you just get so that you long for the sound of another human voice."

"You never told me you get lonely . . ."

"You never asked me . . . anyway, I told her you were at work and I said I didn't know when you'd be back. What time will you be home, anyway?"

"I don't know. I've got something on at the moment. I don't know when it's likely to finish. Could be early, could be late. There's no way of knowing . . ."

"Good job I didn't get the steak and kidney going, isn't it? And by the way, don't bother about the hockey boots. I got a pair."

"You needn't have bothered. I could have got them."

"She needs them tomorrow. You know how embarrassed she is, playing in tennis shoes."

"I'll have to go . . ."

"All right then. I'll leave something in the oven for you, and you'll have to come in the back door. That front-door lock's sticking again. I was wrestling with it all afternoon."

"I'll fix it when I get home . . ."

"Tom's coming round tomorrow to do it . . ."

"I told you, I'll fix it. I told you."

But when I put down the telephone I remembered I'd been telling her I'd fix the front-door lock for over a week.

Sergeant Bates was sitting on the chair in the back corner of the box, the glasses on his knees.

"Shall I start the search?" he said.

I shook my head. "That face. Mean anything to you yet?"

"It's very familiar. I've seen him somewhere. Familiar profile, you know, but it could have been in *Softly, Softly*."

I left him watching, went back to the telephone. Luckily Bill Smythe was still at the station. "Bill you know about locks. Do me a favour . . . On your way home, you practically go past my place. Just have a look at my front-door lock for me, will you? I believe Sarah's having a bit of bother with it. I can make it work all right, but she always seems to get her key jammed, somehow."

"Probably just needs a file running down the side of the key."

"If you could just look at it for me . . ."

I felt better, knowing I'd done something about it.

I went back to Sergeant Bates. Still sitting there, still watching. Not much else we could do. Skelton was in position. Cooper was on his way back to the Hall.

"You see so many faces these days, Inspector, on the television screen."

"You may do, Sergeant, but I don't."

"You ought to watch more, Inspector. Do you good, help you to relax."

"Half my trouble is getting some of you lads unrelaxed. You're sure you can't put a name to him?"

"Absolutely sure, Inspector."

"But you do have the feeling you know him?"

"A vague feeling, yes."

"But you can't say when or where?"

"No, Inspector, I'm afraid I can't."

"Stay there. Don't take your eyes off him."

I touched the concert manager's arm and followed him out of the box. He led me down a flight of stairs, through a door marked PRIVATE, along a subterranean corridor, through a room containing musical instruments, and up a flight of stairs again. When we got to the top we were on the platform, but protected from the audience by a thin screen through which the leader and the conductor went on to the platform. I took the binoculars and focussed them through the slit in the screen, using only one eye. Now I could see him full face. I had been deceived by his semi-profile. His face was not as wide, not as round as I had supposed. And looked at from the front at the same level, his hair didn't show so much.

I knew now where and when I had last seen him.

In court. And what's more, he'd been in the dock.

Only he hadn't been bald, then.

Dammit, they were already into the second movement, and I hadn't even noticed the break.

CHAPTER 4

Joe Habgood and I have been friends for a long time, ever since our time together in the same provincial high school. Now I'm an inspector of police and most of my former school pals are disgusted; but Joe's a feature writer on a newspaper noted for its ability to drop mast first into a vat of manure and come out smelling of violets. Much of its appeal to the "what's been happening while I've been in bed" readership depends on its sub-editing and smart layout. It's the only newspaper you can take in at a glance; the headlines tell all. I was wondering how they would cover this concert if Nameless turned out to be what I thought he was. The switchboard found Joe for me. He was just going off, having put the feature side of the paper to bed for the night.

"Yes, you old bastard, what can I do for you?"

"Joe, this is serious and there's no time, so no clowning, eh?"

"Roger."

"That case at Bow Street, ten, eleven years ago. You and me. We'd been to the Wig and Pen. You thought there might be a possible story."

I remembered the day distinctly. I was off duty. I met Joe about midday at the top of Fleet Street; we knocked a few back at the Wig and Pen, a club at the top of the street opposite the law courts and therefore inhabited by journalists, barristers, and, when we could afford it, off-duty coppers. After our liquid lunch, we crossed the street and went into the law courts. Don't ask me why; you'd think I'd get enough of courts on duty but we went and sat in a press box. Joe thought he might get a feature story out of one of the cases, and we left about four o'clock. A couple of girls were leaving the courts at the same time we were. Joe had a quick eye for a girl in those days, and the voice and tongue of an Irishman. He picked 'em up. Dead simple. They were tourists, from Scandinavia. Social studies and all that. He offered to show them round a newspaper and they lapped it up.

"Joe, it was the day we met those two girls, and we took them over the offices of the *Graphic,* do you remember . . . ?"

"The one with the big . . ."

"I wouldn't know about that. I was married."

"You've always been married in spirit. Okay, I remember. What do you want to know . . . ?"

"We watched a case before the one you thought might interest you. Only half the case, actually. And you said that, since you couldn't find a story in your case, you might do a colour piece on that one. Is this making sense to you?"

"It will do. Let me rummage through the grab bag I jokingly call my memory. I can remember the girls; I was narked because you wouldn't take one of them off my hands—you were always a highly moral bastard . . ."

"One-off sex, who needs it . . . ?"

"We bachelors need it."

"So, get married."

"Now I remember. A little fellow. Round face, clean shaven."

"What was he charged with?"

"Hang on." I heard him flicking a cigarette lighter. "That's better. Too much oxygen getting to my brain. My memory works best in smoke-filled corners and dark holes. No, I can't remember the charge."

"But you can see the face . . . ?"

"Vaguely, but yes, I can see him."

"Who was he, Joe?" I asked.

The line hummed with silence. "Funny thing," he said, "I can remember every hair of that bird's body, but I can't remember a thing about that man. I can remember seeing him standing there in the dock, but as to why he was there, what happened to him, who he was, I just can't remember it . . ."

"Think, Joe, think, dammit!" He knew me too well to take offence, or even to ask me questions.

Silence again. "Sorry," he said, "I think the girl with the knockers has driven him completely out of my mind . . ."

"Try to get him back again will you, Joe. And ring me on this number. . . . And I'm thinking of minutes, not hours . . ." I gave him the number of the telephone kiosk and hung up.

Nameless was still sitting there, still nervously bringing his hand from his lap to his lips. Sergeant Bates was still sitting in the corner, with the glasses to his face, but I knew he was no longer even looking through them. The orchestra was still playing, but I was past hearing or caring. The law courts. Ten, twelve years ago. A lag, I was certain of that. I took the glasses from the sergeant and looked through them, and then, as I focussed on Nameless's face, I tried to picture him again in the dock with hair on the front of his head, and ten years younger. Goddammit. It was in my memory. And it was my job, my bloody job, not to forget.

Look at the man, and wait. Joe will be quick as he can. How I hate waiting. Bates was watching. Skelton was in position, so were the three electricians. Nothing else I could do at the moment, without a name. The name opens doors. If he's a known lag, the name would open the door of the chief inspector's official box of tricks. But what if he wasn't known, or the offence for which he'd been in the dock was something like the misappropriation of company funds, or buggering boy scouts . . .

I rang Sarah again quickly, before Joe came back on the line. Got through first time. "Didn't Susan say *anything?*"

"I've been thinking about her phone call," Sarah said in what I always teasingly called her "think" voice. "Very worrying. I'm sure that girl was bothered about something. Very much on edge, if you know what I mean . . ."

"She's always like that when she has a problem. You'd think it was the end of the world. I've learned to ignore it . . ."

"I don't somehow think you'd ignore this. No, she sounded, well, how can I put it, at the end of her tether."

"But she didn't say anything specific . . . ?"

"No, she asked about you, and I told her, but she seemed as if she wasn't taking it in, somehow."

"You've no idea where she was calling from?"

"It was a call box. She had to keep putting money in. I told her to hang up and I'd call her back, but it was almost as if she didn't hear me."

The hostel had a call box for outgoing calls. It didn't receive incoming calls; they'd had a lot of bother with the phone waking up off-duty nurses who needed sleep more than invitations to sex parties.

"If anything occurs to you, give me a ring, will you?" I read out the number of the kiosk and she wrote it down. It stood in a booth in a passage and no one in the audience would be disturbed by it. What a night to be bothered by Susan. As if I didn't have enough on my plate.

So, the kid was bothered. Sounds as if she's at the end of her tether, Sarah had said. Hell, that was the way she always sounded. Childlike, every emotion a crisis of monumental proportions. I could remember being like that myself, but I got over it by the time I was fifteen. I'd had to. There'd never been anyone to hold my hand, the way I was holding Susan's. Sarah was right, of course, I ought to stop seeing her and let her fend for herself.

Tomorrow, I told myself, I'll break it to her gently tomorrow, tell her she's got to start making her own decisions.

Quick look inside the Hall. Sergeant Bates still sitting there, a solid lump of imperturbability. Working by the book. "Suspect under observation, sir." If I'd said, "Fart, Sergeant," he'd have managed something audible.

What the hell did Sarah mean? Sarah wasn't given to fancies. Not after bringing up two kids, almost unaided by me. . . .

I ought to have kept the line open for Joe, but I couldn't wait.

I dialled the station. "That girl's been here again," the sergeant said, but I didn't answer, asked to be connected to the chief. "I've had a word with Rogers," he said, "but he insists on talking to you." I could hear from the tone of his voice that he was narked by that.

"Rogers can wait, Chief. I was ringing about this man."

"And he can't wait, eh? The station can close down, but your man can't wait . . ."

"I know he's a lag, Chief," I said. And then I waited.

"But you can't put a name to him . . ."

"I remember seeing him in the dock. Bow Street. Ten, eleven years ago."

"What was the charge . . . ?"

Now I felt really sick. "I've forgotten," I was forced to say.

I thought he'd piss himself with mirth at the other end of the line. "You've forgotten THE CHARGE . . . ?"

The man and the charge are always joined in a policeman's mind. Jimmy Wolfingham will always be Jimmy the Con to any policeman who has contact with him. Jack

Wise (G.B.H.—Grievous Bodily Harm). It becomes instinctive. Eggs and bacon, sausage and mash . . .

"I never heard the charge, Chief . . ."

What the hell. It would be useless to explain the circumstances. Each sentence would somehow become another admission of impotence. Each non-fact would be held up for inspection, analysis, derision, and rejection. It'd be shaken for concealed errors, then tossed aside as being of no consequence. He'd make verbal mincemeat of me.

"Look, Chief, please take my word for it. Here's a man in the audience at a concert. I've seen that man in the dock at Bow Street. A letter has been received by the management, and that letter carries no fingerprints which itself is evidence of pre-determination and a certain amount of criminal skill . . ."

"But hardly evidence, eh? Hardly cause enough for me to take men off the beat . . ."

"Yes sir, if you'd please let me finish. I have a hunch . . ."

I could have bitten out my tongue as soon as I had used that word.

He laughed. "A hunch, Armstrong? Who are you now, Sexton Blake or Sherlock Holmes? In the police force, Inspector, we don't have the time or the man-power to run around following hunches. Give me evidence, give me facts, sworn statements, and leave the hunches to the Crime Writers' Association. . . . Look, Armstrong, it's a fact, a readily provable fact—and incidentally I've just had a statement placed on my desk signed by Maurice Brigham which helps to prove this fact—that every time you undertake an investigation the incident becomes, to say the least of it, confused. You have a good record of convictions, I'm not disputing that, but some of the backwash of your cases almost swamps this desk sometimes. You're accident prone, lad, and it's time you accepted that fact. You're a good officer, and I'd hate to lose you, but there are times when I ask myself if I can afford the aspirins you cause me to buy. What you have there is a simple anonymous note. I believe it's part of that student demonstration. It wouldn't take five minutes to bring those students of that Hall and interrogate them, and I don't mind betting you'd get a cough. One of those students planted that note, you mark my words. When you can come to me and tell me that you are convinced, beyond all reasonable doubt, that all the students are entirely innocent, then I'll consider taking further steps.

"Look, lad, I'm not trying to be awkward or pull rank on you. You're an inspector, and that means you have a certain standing. You are in charge of that investigation, and your rank entitles you to conduct it in the manner you see fit. You've got three men to help you, and I know you'll make the best use of them. But I have a responsibility, I have a rank too, and pretty soon I'm going to start asking you for situation reports. I shan't want you telling me 'there's a man with a face I recognise but I don't know his name, he's a criminal but I don't know when or where or what was his crime.'"

I swallowed deep, took my courage in both hands. "Can I have twelve men, Chief, to start a proper search . . . ?"

He laughed at me. "Only twelve? We've got actual crime taking place. Disorderly conduct in Ken High Street, a break-in at Allerton Mansions. Some fellow's beating up his wife in Dobie Street, two cars have crashed near the Park . . . not to mention the backwash of cases you're involved with. Look, Inspector, stop frigging about. Interrogate the students. Search the Hall, and if you have the slighest grounds for suspicion, get everybody out of there in an orderly fashion."

"Very good, Chief. I'll carry on and report to you . . ."

"Do that, Inspector. And now let me get back to crime."

Cooper had returned at last and I met him in the corridor.

"What kept you?"

"I had a sudden thought, Inspector, and remembered a case I once had with a man who looked like our friend in there. I thought I might have a note on my pad."

"And where was your pad, eh lad? Up the chief inspector's arse by the sound of it. . . ." His smile was cheeky but guarded. He didn't know just how far he could go with me. He knew damn well I wasn't the force's favourite, but I could make life harder for him outside the station, down those long cold alleyways in which most of our work seems to happen. "Listen to me, you creep," I said. "When I say 'get back here,' I mean it, not go sloping off to arse lick the chief inspector."

"I don't know what you mean, sir," he said, with a smirk as wide as a choir boy with a comic stuffed under his vestments.

But there was no time to cut this bastard down to size; it would be mean and petty even to try. I opened the door of the box and beckoned for Bates to come out. He bent low so no one would be disturbed by his exit. "Take Cooper and do your best to search the building. I know it's an impossible task for two, so concentrate on the most likely places. You know where."

That was a fallacy, and the way he looked at me showed he realised it. He knew, and I knew, it could be anywhere. Only the previous week a group of angry lads had done a minister's house. A plastic bag, round the S-bend of a lavatory, with enough stuff in it to blow out the entire bog, the bathroom, and the landing.

Mind round the same never-ending cycle; should I be *doing* something? Quizzing the students? Pulling Nameless out of the Hall? Stopping the concert and sending everybody home?

I sat back in the box, the glasses to my eyes, and focussed them again on Nameless. Skelton was still in position, still alert. He was a good lad, the right man for the job, a running jumping laughing lad whom nothing ever bothered. Except cruelty and violence and we get our share of that. Looking at him, I had a sudden idea. I'd let him in on that kid, Rogers. Rogers might cough to Skelton, and it would do Skelton good to work at it. It would also be one in the eye for the chief, who'd said the kid would only cough to me. But I forgot about that—Nameless had moved. He'd bent down and he was fumbling in whatever he had on his lap. You can't switch your mind off, can you? Not just like that. Skelton wasn't married. I'd introduce him to Susan. Skelton half rose in his seat as if stretching his muscles. Yes, introduce him to Susan.

Skelton's hand was flat on the back of the seat in front of him, ready to chop. If it is a bomb, there in the bag . . . If Cooper should find a bomb planted round the S-bend of a lavatory . . . I wasn't worried the building would be blown down. It'd take a hell of a lot of explosive to damage the structure of the building; far more than could be brought in by one man. I wasn't even worried a lot of people would actually be injured by the explosion; Hitler walked away from it when a bomb exploded in his briefing room, didn't he? But bombs make a loud bang, and people are frightened by loud bangs, and they panic. Four thousand people, all panicking, would jam that building, and then we could have a repetition of the tragedy that occurred at a football ground, when an entrance stairway collapsed, and people behind trampled those in front. The lives of people in a crowd are always at risk, depending on the immobility of the mass; once that mass starts moving, few forces on earth can stop it. If any sort of device were to explode in there, no matter how few people the actual device injured, a hundred or more people might be killed in the rush to escape.

Suddenly I remembered I'd ordered the doors locked, thinking to catch anyone sneaking out after he'd planted a device. That had been sloppy, panic thinking. The sergeant and Cooper had started work in the corridor, quickly checking ledges for disturbed dust. I sent Cooper to tell the commissionaires to open all the doors, just in case. Then I went back into the box and stared into the auditorium, my eye automatically going to Nameless. He was still bent over. Christ, what was he doing? Skelton was leaning forward, and now his hand was near his chin, still poised for the chop.

Nameless came upright again. Even with the glasses I couldn't quite make out what he was holding in his hand, but I saw Skelton sit back in his seat and he was close. If you hadn't been watching, you wouldn't realise Skelton had moved. Through the glasses I saw Nameless's hand come higher. It contained a flat box, about the size of a one-pound slab of guncotton. A string hung down the side; was it a decorative ribbon like they put on some boxes, or a fuse cord, or the release mechanism of a detonator? Skelton had given it the all-clear. But I couldn't, not yet. If it was a box of sweets I wanted to see him take one out and eat it. He did just that. Popped a chocolate in his mouth. He had chubby fingers and was wearing a signet ring. His hand moved down again, and the box disappeared from my view. But was it a box of chocolates? *Only* a box of chocolates? Men whose lives depend on their ability to react quickly to another's actions often lose the power of conscious reasoning. Rarely when an incident is over can they relate each step in that event. It happens often when you get the police involved with demonstrations. Somebody starts chucking things, and you go in to try to smother the source of the action. Sometimes you have no alternative but to go in swinging. But when the defence lawyer gets you in the box on a charge of police brutality, you can't always swear truthfully that the long-haired idiot standing in your path had actually offered you violence *before* you went in and through him. You were involved in a series of steps with one final outcome, to stop the man at the back who was chucking bottles. There are procedures, of course, and we all try to live by them, but you can't always stop to think. Skelton hadn't stopped to think, or he might not be so relaxed in his seat. He'd seen what was blatantly a chocolate box and he'd assumed it was a box of chocolates. He'd seen a man eat a chocolate and had assumed there was nothing but chocolates in the box.

But wasn't that what I myself was doing? Making assumptions from insufficient visual evidence? An anonymous note, a nameless man I had recognised, and a smell, a hunch. But so far as the police were concerned, I'd already started the wheels in motion. I'd devoted time, and men, to an investigation. It was in the sergeant's book as an incident. Was I going to have to draw a line across the sergeant's page and say, incident closed, sorry I made a fool of myself? I'm a man of instincts. I could start a police car and chase a man at ninety miles an hour, and stop him before he got to the air terminal. But I can never tell you afterwards how many bollards I've driven round the wrong way. I can walk into a man who's holding a knife and take it off him every time, but couldn't tell you at what moment I decide to drop my arm and make my feint to get in under the blade.

"For God's sake do something," I muttered to Nameless. "Give me a start point. Anything. Anything."

The concert manager touched my shoulder. I put down the glasses and turned to him.

"I've been thinking . . ."

I nodded.

"That man you're watching. The one we've got the lights aimed at . . ."

I nodded again.

"He may not be the one . . ."

I could have groaned. "I know that. I'm having the building searched, just in case."

"It's a big building to search . . ."

"They're two of my best men. Specialists . . ."

"But do they know what they're looking for?"

"Don't worry. It's a thing we often have to do."

We look for the non-obvious, the thing that's right and wrong, the oddity. The Germans taught us a lot with their booby traps towards the end of the last war. They'd leave a dolly on a window ledge, and a soldier'd pick it up, intending to take it home for his kid. If ever he got home again. The dolly'd be stuffed full of explosives. That was only one of their tricks, and they had hundreds.

I put the glasses on Nameless again. He hadn't moved. Skelton was on balance again.

The manager wouldn't let me alone. "I really think you ought to get more men here, stop the concert, and clear the Hall."

"We haven't *got* any more men," I hissed. The minute I'd said it I realised how lame it sounded. We needed a hundred men, and for that we'd need to start our "snowball" system. Dead easy, really, and it works fast. We ring one man, and he has three numbers to ring before he leaves home. Each of those three numbers has three other numbers to ring. And so the calls snowball. Of course, not all the men we ring are at home, but we get a high percentage, and when absolutely necessary we can put a hundred police, firemen, and heavy gang contractors men on location within fifteen minutes.

But "snowball" requires top authority and the man with access to that authority was sitting on a heap of crime. The chief had to deploy his available men to best advantage, and I wasn't giving him much information to justify pulling in the beat men, ringing round other divisions, or calling in off-duty men.

"I thought you had lots of men at the station," James Barrett said.

"We also have lots of crime . . ."

"If anything should happen to frighten that audience . . ."

I'd been on duty once at a football match when the stand caught fire. I didn't need Barrett to tell me about frightened audiences.

This time they made me wait before they connected me with the chief, and they didn't try to pass any messages to me. When he came on the line he had that "well, what do you want now" weariness in his voice.

"Making my first situation report, Chief. I'd like to report we have four thousand people here in this Hall. If the crowd should try to get through the exits in a panic . . ."

"You know the answer to that. Stop the concert, and make a search."

They pay chief inspectors to be right. "Listen to me, Inspector," he said. "You've gone to investigate an anonymous note. We receive many anonymous notes and not one of 'em has turned out to mean anything for the past few years, but quite properly we've investigated them. But until you can turn up something more tangible than a face in the crowd you think you recognise, I can't give you any more help. The procedures are quite clear. If you have any legitimate ground for suspicion you have the authority to do what is necessary to stop that concert and clear that Hall. Until then I must remind you that I have a station to run, and I can't run it from a box in the Royal Hall."

I could hear his other telephone ringing, heard him pick it up, and the clink as the two mouthpieces came together. He had three telephones on his desk, one a "hot line" with an unlisted number. I knew the problems: a sprawling map spread on the wall before you, a festering sore of violence and corruption, an anti-social volcano constantly erupting with man's inhumanity to man. The radio crackles constantly in the ops room but every incident however small eventually finds its way to the figure-head, the can-carrier. Most police incidents are small domestic fracases, insignificant in themselves, petty theft, motor vehicle collisions, traffic snarls; but somewhere in the middle is the one man with a knife he has no intention of using until someone stupidly provokes him, or the suicide who doesn't want to die and craves to tell someone he's swallowed a bottle of pills before the creeping numbness overtakes him. Every copper knows the feeling of looking at a map and saying to himself "out there two or three people will die simply because we can't get to them in time." Old folks with no one to care fall down a flight of steps, and lie there while a milkman puts three weeks of milk outside; men of hope and promise drive carefully down a road and are knocked to kingdom come by a layabout, driving a stolen van with no brakes, leaving the police to tell his wife and wide-eyed kids, "No, I won't have a cup of tea, thank you; I'm very sorry but I have to inform you your man is dead."

"I'll ring you back, Chief," I said. I'd just seen Sergeant Bates out of the corner of my eye, beckoning to me. Cooper was with him. I hung up the phone and ran. Next to the refreshment room was a small alcove. In it, against the wall, was one of those cone-shaped fire extinguishers. An instruction card was tied to the neck below the striking plunger which protruded from the top protected by a lift-off mesh cage. The paintwork was pristine, but there was a bright gleam of metal on the ring below the plunger. Someone had taken the top off it recently, and hadn't used the proper equipment.

Fire extinguishers in public places are examined regularly. A man like James Barrett would see the law was rigidly applied. But whoever'd had the top off that extinguisher hadn't used the correct tool.

"Get Barrett, quickly," I whispered to Cooper. I bent down and looked at the ring. The top must have been difficult to take off. It had been twisted with a Stilson wrench; I could see the bite of the Stilson's teeth. The extinguisher stood in a ring of moisture that could be seepage. The ring was wider than the extinguisher. I traced the ring on the floor with my finger.

"That's what caught my eye," Sergeant Bates said. "Another extinguisher standing there for a long time, wider than this one. From the dampness of that stain, I'd say this extinguisher was put there fairly recently."

It's too damned easy to remove a piece of equipment from a public building. Three men walked through the front doors of a broadcasting studio wearing brown coats and pulling a trolley. They walked out again with a Bluethner piano that's never been seen since. The commissionaire on duty held the door open for them. "I thought they were from the piano tuners," he said afterwards. Someone could have walked in here, walked out again with an extinguisher under his arm. "I'm just taking it to fill it," he'd say, and perhaps the doorman would hold the door open for *him*. Once outside, he could fill it with what he liked. Or else he could already have had an extinguisher under his arm when he came in, stolen from a cinema or somewhere. And already primed. Who'd suspect a man who walks *into* a public building with a fire extinguisher, puts it down, and takes one out? People don't *steal* fire extinguishers.

Barrett arrived. "These extinguishers . . . ? What can you tell me about 'em?"

He looked blank. "Who's responsible for them?"

"The maintenance staff," he said.

"When were they last serviced?"

"I don't know. I can't see to everything myself, you know . . ."

The sergeant had twisted the card, gingerly.

"Doesn't it tell you there?" Barrett asked, and almost put his hand on the knob to tilt the extinguisher so that we could read the card more easily. I knocked his hand away. Then the penny dropped.

"Is that it? Is there something in it . . . ?" He stood there, not quite rigid, but not moving.

"Who would be responsible for servicing them?" I asked him.

"We have a service contract with the firm who supplies them. I'd have to talk to the maintenance engineer."

"Where's he?"

"In the boilerhouse, I imagine. He always stays on duty during a concert . . ."

"Get him," I said to the sergeant. "No, on second thoughts, go down to the boilerhouse with Mr. Barrett and find out exactly when these extinguishers were last serviced. You, Cooper, get on to the sergeant at the station—the sergeant, mark you, not the chief inspector—and give him a preliminary warning for the Army."

The sergeant and Barrett had already hurried away; Cooper followed them down the corridor.

It would be dead easy. Fill the extinguisher with explosive. Fit a detonator and a delayed action fuse into the top. Then bring in the extinguisher and exchange it for one already standing here. We wouldn't have spotted it if they hadn't been different sizes, and the previous one hadn't leaked over the years. Then come back for the concert; wait until a crowd was milling about in this corridor, stand yourself in front of the extinguisher. Who notices what one man is doing in a crowd? You'd lift off the protective covering, and press down the plunger to fire the delayed action fuse. Walk slowly away, don't run, don't do anything to attract attention to yourself. One, two, three minutes or hours or days later, depending on the timing of that fuse, the extinguisher would explode. It'd kill anyone standing along this corridor, but it'd probably also blow out this wall and then its blast would go into the Hall itself, injuring hundreds. These extinguisher cases are made of tempered steel, each fragment a deadly missile when the extinguisher explodes. The panic in the crowd would be instantaneous. There'd probably be fire to add to the panic.

Sergeant Bates came back, Barrett steaming beside him.

"There was a telephone call from your wife as I was passing the box," Sergeant Bates said, "but I told her you were busy."

"Thanks. What about the extinguishers . . . ?"

"They were all serviced, just this afternoon. The maintenance man knows the lad who did it. He'd been doing it every six months for donkey's years. They play chess together?"

"And the marks?"

"The service engineer had had his C spanner pinched. They used a Stilson wrench. It slipped and the maintenance man's got a nasty bruise on his finger."

Some things you believe, some you don't. I could see the sergeant believed this, had written off the extinguisher as a source of potential danger. I lifted the plunger protector, and grasped the ring. It had been greased, and it turned in my hand with only a slight pressure. I unscrewed it and lifted it out. Beneath it was the acid capsule, a glass phial hanging in the soda liquid. There was no sign of any other mechanism. . . .

Barrett waited until we were out of the hearing of Sergeant Bates, who carried on with his search, before he himself exploded. "Inspector," he said, "I think you are out of your depth in this investigation. You should send for your superior officer. We should empty the Hall and search it properly."

That was the one thing reason told me to do, but instinct insisted I could not do. If there was someone in that Hall who had prepared something, some way of killing another person, or persons, then for me to start to clear the Hall would, could make him panic and do whatever he had come here to do. It was as simple as that. If he was holding a gun and we walked on to the stage to stop the concert, ten to one, no a hundred to one, he'd fire the gun. If it was a knife, he'd stick it in somebody. And if it was a bomb, he'd set it off. I knew that, in my bones. But I couldn't explain it in a way that would convince even my own chief inspector and he has as sharp an instinct as any policeman I know. I doubted if I'd even convinced Sergeant Bates or Cooper, and they were in the Hall with me and any atmosphere of danger should have communicated itself to them. Meanwhile, Skelton was down there on his own, nursing the one man on whom, quite without evidence, I'd fixed my suspicions.

I ought to have called for the help of the commissionaires. I ought to have had them watching Skelton for me, ready to go to his assistance should he move. But I have a rooted aversion from using civilians in a police investigation; they're too eager, too well meaning, too conscious of an opportunity of playing at coppers. And what we needed at that moment was cold professional ability in a potentially dangerous situation. I wanted absolute control, and I couldn't get that if I used amateurs.

I went back into the box, Barrett following, his question unanswered. I don't really think he expected an answer, he was making administrative noises. I trained the glasses along the back of the rows I could see in the upper floors. Cooper and Bates were working their way along, checking fire extinguishers, doors, windows, abutting the Hall, backs of seats, fronts of seats, ventilator grilles, air shafts, suspended microphones.

Suspended microphones. The BBC box was empty, the lights out, since the concert was not being broadcast; but the microphones had been left hanging all over the Hall.

The switchboard at the BBC connected me immediately with the duty officer, and he rapidly found a studio manager. A bright young man, he asked no superfluous questions once I had identified myself and had told him where I was. "Those microphones, hanging in the Hall, what do they do?"

"One set picks up the orchestra, the other set picks up applause, crowd reactions, and the orchestra's reverberations."

"Can they be turned on easily?"

"Yes, they're permanently connected to the mixer."

"Where's that?"

"In the BBC box."

"Who has the key?"

"There's one at the Royal Hall."

"Do you have a key to the BBC box?" I asked Barrett. He held up a ring of keys and indicated one. "We've got the key," I said. "Now how do we switch on the microphones?"

I heard him cup the telephone in his hand, and speak on another line. "Go into the BBC box," he said, "and on the broadcasting desk you'll find a built-in telephone. Not the ordinary telephone on the top of the desk, but the one hanging at the side. Pick that up, and I hope you'll find me at the other end of it."

We went into the BBC box together. The manager drew the curtains before we switched on the light. The telephone on the top of the table was green, the other one grey. I picked it up.

"Jolly good, it's worked," I heard the studio manager say.

I looked at the bank of instruments in front of me. Many small wheels, all marked with a number. To the left of the dashboard was a meter, and a larger wheel, almost two inches in diameter, below that. The studio manager on the other end of the telephone told me how to switch on the apparatus. It warmed up almost instantly and filled the box with sound. Even he could hear it at the other end of the telephone line. "Turn the large fader," he said, "the master fader," but then he remembered my ignorance, and directed my hand towards the large wheel, which I turned to the left until the meter needle read four. Now the music and the audience were both audible. Acting to his instructions, I was able either to reduce the sound of the orchestra or the sound of the audience, listening selectively to each part of the Hall in turn. He too was listening. "I've had control room plug me through," he said. "We have a permanent music line to the Royal Hall."

As I turned up each fader, from the quality of the sound it produced he was able to identify the microphone to which it was attached. "That one's directly over the conductor's head," he said. I looked and saw what looked like a metal bottle, hanging ten feet above Flughafer's head, but a little behind him so that, should it fall, it would not crown him. "That one's at the very back of the Hall," he said, when I turned the first fader down and brought up another, "and I would say it's quite low down." It was. About fifteen feet above the back row of the audience. Another one was high up, in the ceiling.

When I turned up fader four, there was no sound.

"Disconnected," he said. "Turn up five." I did. "Incidentally," he said, "I've asked one of our studio managers to come round to the Royal Hall in case you need anything. If the traffic's all right and she can get a taxi, she'll be with you in less than ten minutes."

Finally, we were all set. At the flick of a fader, I could

listen to any part of the Hall; with the audience microphone, I could detect the whispering animal sounds of the crowd, the snufflings, the rustle of clothing, tense and stiff limbs being relaxed in chair-creaking movements. Or I could focus on the orchestra itself, isolating each section with great clarity. I hadn't the faintest idea what I wanted to hear, and how quickly I could construe what I did hear, but somehow I felt a greater confidence now I had ears in every part of the Hall. I switched off the light and opened the curtains. Ears and eyes. From the darkened and soundproofed interior I could see the entire Hall, and listen to any part of it.

"We're all set," I said to the studio manager.

"Do me a favour and leave the master fader open, will you, I'm nosy by nature."

That gave me my first laugh of the evening. Talking with him had been a stimulant, and the intense unfamiliar action of setting up the studio had clarified my thoughts like a whiff of menthol. There was nothing I could do, except sit and watch. I'd made my preparations, and now it was up to the man in the audience to make his move. I could relax.

So, watching the unnamed man, and listening to the orchestra playing, I used the second telephone in the box to ring Sarah.

"It was nothing you could put your finger on," she said, "but I've been thinking about your Susan. I wish you'd try to get in touch with her."

"But you told me you thought I ought to stay away from her."

"Yes, but that was before I talked with her. I'd like you to try to get hold of her, if only for my own peace of mind. It's nothing you could put your finger on, like I said, just a suspicion."

"I spend half my life acting on suspicions," I said, to reassure her.

The hostel was in West Central Division. Who did I know there? Arthur Charles. Arthur would help me. I rang West Central, got him first try.

"What do you want, you old sod," he said. "Haven't seen you in ages. Did you get that pusher I put you on to . . . ?"

"Haven't time to chat, Arthur. Can you do something for me. Not official. Can you send one of your girls round to the nurses' hostel at St. Brigits. Look for a girl called Susan Reynolds. See if she's got any problems . . ."

"Nothing official?"

"No, it's a sort-of a welfare case I've got mixed up in . . ."

"Does your wife know . . . ?" Arthur chuckled, though I could detect the serious note.

"What do you take me for, Arthur . . . ?"

"Never figured you for a chaser . . ."

"I'm not. It's not like that. Will you do it, unofficially?"

"I'll send a girl round, out of uniform."

"Thanks a million."

I gave him the telephone number in the corridor. It seemed to me so many people now had that number, but the one man I wanted to use it was late. What the hell was keeping Joe all this time . . . ? No use me ringing him; he'd come through as soon as he had anything to tell me.

Sergeant Bates came into the box. "Negative on the ground floor," he said, "even the lavatories. Cooper's all wet and mad as hell . . ."

"Cooper's always been all wet, and a constable has no right to get mad . . ."

"Oh, by the way, there was a call for you from a man called Joe, but he said it was personal and I said you were too busy to come to the phone."

I was glad to be in a sound-proof box the way I swore at him.

Joe was waiting for my call and had obviously alerted the switchboard. They put me straight through.

"You won't like this," he said, "that man . . ."

As he began to speak my memory did one of those tricks and leaped back ten years.

". . . was shouting at the Judge—Jophs—when they put him down. . . ."

I could see the scene again, that face distorted with anger as he yells from the steps down into the cells, Mr. Justice Jophs looking inscrutable as ever from the Bench, and the rest of the court in uproar.

"I've looked up my notes and the back issues," Joe said, but I no longer needed him.

"He was put away for fifteen years," I said. "He tried to blow up a girls' school . . ."

"The *Mirror* made up a name for him."

"The Mad Bomber. Mad Mike Harrigan."

Our desk sergeant back at the station was alert. "Everything you can get for me on Mad Mike Harrigan, sent down at the law courts just over ten years ago for a fifteen. I don't know the exact charge."

In ten minutes I'd have the lot. Physical characteristics, past history, but most important, *modus operandi.* How does he prefer to do it? Criminals fall into patterns. Crime's a nerve-racking business; you can hardly blame 'em for deriving what comfort they can from a regular routine. Soon I'd know if he'd often used a bomb, what kind of bomb it'd be, did he plant it or chuck it, what explosive did he use. Did he go for blast without much solid matter, or a lot of flying metal that can slice its way through a crowd like a hot knife through butter? Did he add incendiary materials; would we have fire and burns in addition to all the broken bones? How was he on fuses? Reliable? If he'd set the bomb for 2112 hours, at which time the Choral Symphony would end, did I have that much time to find it, or might it explode any time after, say, 2030?

This time the chief inspector didn't sneer.

"Mad Mike Harrigan. Bomb in a girls' school, about eleven years ago, sent down for a fifteen . . . ?" He was good, no doubt about it. He was good where I should have been, in memory.

"You're certain of the identification?"

"Yes, Chief, that's one thing I'm sure of."

He didn't pick up the lead, didn't sneer.

"You've got him covered?" he asked.

"Yes. Skelton's in the next row, one seat to the side."

"Good," he said. "I'll get on to the Army . . ."

"I've already sent 'em a preliminary alert."

"Good, good. I'll activate it. I'll be right over. You, meanwhile, stop the concert and clear the Hall."

He hung up.

There it was again. "Stop the concert." That's all anybody could say. Walk out on to that platform and lift your hands. Flughafer would stop, certainly, make the move with his baton that would cut the orchestra in mid-bar. Then he'd look puzzled at whoever had walked on to the platform. Meanwhile, conversation would have started in the audience. "Who is he? What's happened? What's it all about?"

One man in that audience at that moment would know quite clearly what it was all about, but the chanches are he wouldn't be talking to his neighbour. He'd either sit there, smug, knowing his fuse was timed to explode in ten minutes, or, and this was why I couldn't stop the concert, he'd take that as his cue, press the detonator on his bomb and either sit on it or get up and walk away from it. Either way, metaphorically speaking, that bomb would be ticking, and

I was damned certain we would not be able to find it in time.

What do we *do* when we receive that first urgent telephone call of a multiple car crash, a man holed up in a house with a shotgun, a heavily armed gang robbing a bank, a petrol tanker involved in a street accident and leaking, and unexploded bomb in a public place?

Most police stations keep a Procedures Book that deals with all possible eventualities; it contains everything a policeman coping with such an incident will need to know. The page marked "Bombs in Public Places" started by saying "remove all members of the public," and then carried on with a carefully compiled check-list of things to do. The interview room at the station was immediately set up as an incidents room and Inspector Burroughs of the uniformed branch was put in charge of it. He drew a new foolscap lined book from stores, and wrote on the cover ROYAL HALL and an incident number. From that moment everything that happened, every telephone call, every message, was entered into that book.

The Procedures Book said, "Ring the Army."

"Major Watkins here."

"Inspector Burroughs, D Division. You've already had a preliminary warning, I believe, about the Royal Hall."

"That's right. We're standing by. Any info yet?"

"No, but we think it could be a home-made bomb."

"They're the worst."

"How soon can you be there?"

"One minute."

The divisional chief superintendent looked at a map of the area, a large detailed police map. On it, clearly marked, was every gas main, every electric line, post office telephone line, water main, and several communication lines coded top secret. All these lines passed dangerously close to the Royal Hall. "Damn," he said.

Certain properties were coloured: the residences of VIPs, embassies, legations, consulates. "Damn," he said again.

"Inspector Armstrong's handling this, you say?" he asked the superintendent standing with him.

"Yes, he's on his own."

"Damn," the chief superintendent said, a third time. "You've no idea what type of explosive he suspects? And how much?"

"Could be a briefcase full."

"A briefcase full of what? Gunpowder? Sugar and sulphur, charcoal and potassium nitrate bought from a chemist? Gelignite pinched from a quarry? Plastic, from an army depot?"

"We don't know."

"We can't take a chance. Get everybody out of these flats. Clear the roads. You know what to do."

"One minute? That's damn quick, from Shepherd's Bush."

"We're not at Shepherd's Bush. I moved on the preliminary warning. I've got my chaps in a pick-up truck, parked at the bottom of Beacon Gardens. In wireless contact."

"Marvellous. Message timed, 2035hrs, reference RH/RE/2."

"Roger and out."

MESSAGE RH/INF/19.
Superintendent Greaves to RH/ETA/2036.

No action required. Timed 2035hrs

MESSAGE RH/INT/22
Chief Inspector Roberts at RH. Will wait for superintendent before contacting Inspector Armstrong or entering building.

No action required. Timed 2035hrs

ACTION: RH/4
House clearance ordered on map perimeter A as per PB.
ACTION: Inspectors Pemberton, Tewsley, Fibre, Rinsdale
Signed: Burroughs 2036hrs

ACTION: RH/5
Traffic amendments on pattern TA as per PB.
ACTION: Superintendent Beasley.
Signed: Burroughs 2036hrs

The building was divided into five "luxury" flats and overlooked the Royal Hall. "I'll take the top flat," Inspector Fibre said to Sergeant Timpson, "you take the fourth floor, and we'll leapfrog each other."

"They aren't going to like it," the porter said.

The American went to the bedroom door and called, "Martha, get in here, will you?" She was extremely attractive, in her early thirties, the inspector would have estimated.

"This is Inspector Fibre from the local police," the American said. "He's told me somebody's planted a bomb in the Royal Hall."

She didn't turn a hair.

"May have planted a bomb," the inspector said.

"They're evacuating the folks all around . . ."

Martha looked quickly round the room. "We'll take the Brueghel, the emeralds, in fact all my jewellery."

"Where do you suggest we go, Inspector?"

"We'll check into a hotel," Martha said, strictly no nonsense. Already she was lifting a framed drawing from the wall. "You realise our insurance specifically includes civil action, war, acts of God," she said.

"What's going on, Superintendent?" the man said, leaning out of the window of his Rolls.

"I'm afraid this road is blocked to traffic, sir," the superintendent said. "Your driver will have to follow the diversion signs."

"But I live just there, by the Royal Hall."

"Ah, yes, in that case, sir, I wonder if I could ask you to pull over to the kerb while my inspector has a word with you . . ."

The superintendent beckoned the inspector forward.

"Another resident," he said.

"He'll want to go in and get his valuables . . ."

"He can't, I'm afraid."

"He'll make a fuss about his wife, if he has one."

"Tell him she's been instructed to telephone the station. If he cares to telephone, he'll get news of her . . ."

"Do you think it's a bomb, Superintendent?"

"It's not up to us to speculate, Inspector, so get about your business."

The dispatcher ran into the nurses' canteen. A group of male nurses were taking supper together. The dispatcher ran up to the table, stood there panting.

"You need more exercise," Paddy said.

"How many of you can drive an ambulance?" the dispatcher said when he got his breath back.

Four of them said yes, they could drive an ambulance. One of them said he could drive a car and he supposed there wasn't much difference in driving an ambulance, was there?

"Right lads, report to the dispatch office right away."

"Right away? You mean after supper," Paddy said, always the barrack-room lawyer.

"We've got an emergency on. Probably need every ambulance in West London. And there isn't time to bring in the drivers."

"Bad as that, is it?"

"What is it, an earthquake . . . ?"

"A motor-car pile up . . . ?"

"A fire in a cinema . . . ?"

"No lads, a bomb in the Royal Hall, and they've got a full house of over four thousand people . . ."

"Jesus Christ . . ."

"Let's pray he's one of 'em."

"... We shall want—here, I've got a list—five three-ton lorries, three Drotts, whatever they may be, three J.C.B.s, and at leasty fifty men, with thirty picks and fifty shovels. One air compressor with three jack hammers and three by a hundred yards of compression hosing, and whatever lifting gear you can manage, up to fifty tons."

"Is that all?"

"That's what it says on the list."

"Right. I've got it. Now, where's the site?"

"The Royal Hall."

"The . . . Royal . . . Hall."

"And who did you say all this was to be booked out to . . . ?"

"The Home Office . . ."

"Very well. Is there a reference . . . ?"

"Yes, hold on, here it is, HO/MP/EF/RH/169, and my name is Burroughs, Inspector."

"Very good, Inspector Burroughs. It sounds like a bloody mess you've got down there, but our lads'll sort it out. They'll have that bit of ground flat as a parking lot within a couple of hours . . ."

"I hope not . . . the bomb hasn't gone off yet."

The number rang, and rang, and rang. I was about to put down the telephone when I heard the instrument lifted at the far end.

"Who is there?" a voice asked, a quavering uncertain voice unaccustomed to speaking on a telephone. I could judge its owner to be at least a hundred and fifty years old.

"This is the police," I said, articulating slowly and clearly with a forlorn hope of getting through first time. "Please may I speak to the judge, as quickly as possible?"

"The police," the voice said. Male or female? It was impossible to tell. "What did you want?"

"I want to speak to Mr. Justice Jophs. It's extremely urgent."

"Oh, it's urgent?"

"That's right. Can you ask him to come to the telephone?"

"I'm afraid I cannot do that."

There was a pause.

"Why can't you do that?"

"Because the judge is not here."

"Where is the judge?"

"I'm afraid he's gone out for the evening."

"Where has he gone to?"

"No, I'm afraid the judge is out for the evening." Again there was a pause.

"Can you tell me where the judge has gone?"

"Who did you say you are? Mr. Polis?"

"The police. I know the judge is out. Can you tell me where he has gone?"

"I don't expect to see him back until about eleven o'clock. Shall I leave a note to tell him you called? I'm so sorry you've missed him, but you see he's not here."

"Please can you tell me where he's gone?"

"Oh, didn't I say?" He chuckled. "I must be becoming forgetful. He's gone to a concert at the Royal Hall."

CHAPTER 5

Barrett was standing beside me in the BBC box. "Why do you want to telephone a judge?" he said. "I thought you were involved in this anonymous note business . . ."

"If you wanted to find one person in this audience, how would you do it?" I asked him. He thought for a moment. Give him credit, when you asked him a question with an answer that could be unlocked from his mental files he was quick.

"One, check at the box office. Tickets booked by telephone all have names attached to them. Two, check the patrons' list to see if the name you want is on it. Three, check the boxes . . ."

"Is Mr. Justice Jophs a patron? J-O-P-H-S?"

"Not to my knowledge."

"Do you know the names of all of them?"

"I think so. Jarman, Jebbs, Jimpson, Jimpson-Smith, Jones Sir Bartlett, Jones Henry, ones Llewellyn, The Jupiter Trust, Jurgens . . . no Jophs, I'm afraid. I can check the booking office for you . . ."

"Please."

Cooper came into the box. "You're wanted on the phone," he said. "I was passing by on my way to the first-floor lavatories and heard it ring."

"Right." I assumed it was the chief. It wasn't.

"That girl I sent round to the nurses' hostel," Arthur said, "she's just phoned in and can't find any trace of your friend."

"Well, thanks for the effort, Arthur. I'll buy a drink sometime. In a bit of a hurry at the moment."

"Hang on, there's more. So my girl, being bright, nosed about a bit. Talked to a few of the nurses. Apparently this Susan of yours has been a bit of a worry lately. Real down in the mouth, if you know what I mean. Depressed."

"All girls get like that sometimes . . ."

"Ah, but this was a bit more than usual."

"What does that mean . . . ?"

"Well, just that they were all bothered about her. So my girl's gone looking for her. All unofficial, you understand, just helping out."

Arthur was a good sort. He didn't need a Rule Book. "That's very good of you, Arthur, I do appreciate that. But I've got to break off now. I think we've got a U.B. In the Royal Hall."

"I saw it on the tape . . . rather you than me."

You go to the box office to buy a ticket for a concert. You can go to a booking agency. Or you can send someone to either place to do it for you. No one needs to know your name. People buy tickets and then give them away and the name of the person using the ticket is not recorded anywhere. No reason why it should be.

Sergeant Bates was sitting by the control panel looking out.

"Have you ever come up against Judge Jophs?"

"I'm afraid not, Inspector."

"Then you don't know what he'd look like?"

"I didn't say that, Inspector. I've seen his picture."

"Without the wig?"

"Yes . . ."

"Then get busy with the glasses. I think he's somewhere in the Hall and I want him found. That man down there is Mad Mike Harrigan. When they sent him down he threatened to do the judge. He's not been out very long. This could be his night for paying old scores."

The sergeant trained the glasses through the window of the box, and started to sweep the rows with them.

"Try the boxes first," I suggested. I didn't imagine that, on a judge's pay, there was much point in searching the gallery. . . .

James Barrett returned with the booking plan and the booking notes and we went out into the corridor to read them. The plan was clearly printed with names, the notes were barely legible. Not one of them in any way resembled the word JOPHS, though there had been many erasures. I didn't have much hope of finding his name on the plan. Barrett took the plan back to the front office and I went and sat in the empty box next to the BBC box. On my own. To think. Within minutes they'd all be here, the chief inspector, the constables and sergeants borrowed from Division, the fire brigade, the ambulance service. Then we'd get the brass: the superintendent, the assistant commissioner, perhaps even the commissioner himself if he was in London. And the Army, the Royal Engineers.

And they'd all be after my blood. "Inspector, why haven't you cleared the Hall? Why haven't you pulled out Harrigan? Why . . . ?"

The BBC Radio. *Radio*. If it was a bomb, it could be anywhere, not necessarily in Harrigan's bag. And he could operate it with a *radio*-controlled device. Damn it, they fly model airplanes up to a mile away with a radio set, don't they? And that radio-controlled device could be in his bag.

Once again I looked at Mad Mike, Skelton poised behind him. In every portion of my being I felt that whether the note were genuine or not, Harrigan was the key to any danger that might exist in that auditorium. And Harrigan was a nutter. I couldn't run the risk of provoking him, in his madness, to activate whether by hand or by radio a device I felt in my bones was hidden somewhere in that place.

The music had taken on a bittersweet air, moving inexorably from bar to bar with a verve and line that at any other time would have excited me beyond measure. Now it was like some ghastly metronome, a timing device that was counting off the seconds to a blast that could have everyone panicking in the aisles, jamming the doorways. A love of classical music is no badge of courage. If a bomb blew, or a gun was fired, the people in that Hall would behave as crowds do everywhere, everytime. I knew we had to find the bomb, the gun, whatever device had been placed as an instrument of death. So far, all my money was on a bomb. I was sure it was a bomb, and that Mad Mike was somehow responsible.

But then again, thinking about it, I realise I'd built convincing arguments of nothing but suspicion and an anonymous note which experience told me I could discount. I could build the same tower of suspicion about anything. Susan for example; three people had given me evidence which *could* be interpreted to suggest Susan was off-balance. Damn it, if I didn't take control of myself I'd be building Susan up into being a suicide. . . .

Stick to the case in hand. If it is a case. Mad Mike. What's known about him? Bomb in a girls' school, fifteen years inside after threatening a judge. He'd served ten years. Anonymous note received. Who sent it? Was Mad Mike working with somebody? Had they fallen out? Mad Mike was a loner. I was certain of that. There'd be no accomplice to grass on him.

Mad Mike himself had sent that note. Sitting at his kitchen table, perfecting his bomb, constructing it with the utmost care, he'd have thought of a way to make his revenge complete. At some point in his tortuous thinking, he'd have decided to send a note. Tell 'em all about it, in advance, the gesture of a typical nutter. "Think," I said to myself, "like a nutter!" Two possibilities. Either you want the tremendous unleashing of power that only causing an explosion can give you, or you want to use an explosive device to kill someone. You're not concerned with what will happen to other people. You're not really aware of the existence of other people. You want one person to be killed. Or you want to cause a big bang. If you want to kill somebody with a bomb, where would you plant it? If you wanted to make a big bang, how would you do that?

Harrigan was sitting downstairs. Madmen don't sit downstairs, they go high, stand on balconies, climb on ledges, climb, always climb. To make a big bang Harrigan would place himself in the gallery where he could look down with the Hall spread out below, ant-like figures scurrying to their seats, minuscule humans awaiting his wrath and vengeance. But Harrigan was sitting *with* them, in the stalls, with the weight of the Hall, the loaded terraces and boxes, the balconies above him. And he was munching sweets. I saw him pop yet another into his mouth at that moment and start to chew on it. So, the big bang was out, except as an incidental to his main purpose, which was to kill somebody.

Mr. Justice Jophs. Of that I felt quite certain.

But where was the judge?

If only I could produce the judge for the chief inspector and the brass hats, perhaps I might get off the hook for not clearing the Hall. They might listen to me and not insist on the Hall being cleared.

I went back into the BBC box.

"Any luck, Sergeant?"

"Not yet."

"I'm going to the front door. Keep looking, but come to me if you spot him."

"And if I don't?"

"Remember to tell the brass, when they ask, you suggested that I should clear the Hall."

On the way to the front door I met Cooper drying his hands. "Report to Sergeant Bates in the BBC box," I said. "He'll tell you what to do."

He flashed me a look of pure hatred. There are at least a hundred lavatories in the Royal Hall, and he'd been down 'em all.

Three cars outside the Hall; nine men in them waiting for the chief inspector. A fourth car arrived, a fifth. It was a cool night, clear but crisp. No clouds. At least, not in the sky. I glanced at my watch, imagined them calling in "on station outside the Royal Hall" and then the time. A laconic "message received" in reply, and then a repeat of the time. It's all commonplace to people who watch *Z Cars*.

The fire brigade control vehicle arrived, a Zodiac, painted fire-engine red, its light flashing but its siren dead. It parked and waited.

We were all waiting.

Standing on the front step I could hear nothing of the music. The flow of "civilians" had been halted and no cars passed along the road south of the Park. Somewhere round the back of the Royal Hall a van would be travelling, dropping constables off at the intersections. The incidents officer would have a large-scale map of the area and he'd draw ring "A" round the Hall and prepare to evacuate every building within that ring. Not because of the primary explosion, but because of the gas mains and the secondary fires. They'd divert traffic through the Park and up Church Street, alert a civilian contractor to stand by with lorries, bulldozers, gangs with picks and shovels. Soon the ambulances would begin to arrive to take casualties to beds in hospitals throughout London. What was left of the casualties, the ones they couldn't piece together for identification, would go to the local mortuary and the forensic boys would play jigsaws with them.

All this activity of preparation because I had recognised

a face in the crowd and an anonymous note had been received.

The chief inspector's car drew up at the front door of the Hall and he got out. His car drove away and parked with the others. Sergeant Dobbs was with him and Constable Keegan, our whiz kid from records. The chief inspector stood still as I walked across to him. He looked at me without speaking. I looked back. It wasn't a moment for saying "Nice evening."

"Inspector Burroughs is incident officer," the chief said, "and by now the Post Office should have plugged the switchboard lines from the Royal Hall through to him. The chief superintendent is on his way. I notice that, despite my instructions which I thought were quite specific, you haven't started clearing the Hall. Not much point in my saying the chief superintendent will have your balls for that but he will you know."

"I could resign, if you want me to."

"Be your age," he said. "They'll want to see blood before they'll let you resign."

"And you . . . ?"

"You're lucky. I still have an open mind."

Constable Keegan had brought two pairs of binoculars with him. He gave me one, the chief inspector the other, and we walked round inside the Hall to the BBC box.

"Any luck?" I asked Sergeant Bates, who'd risen to his feet when he saw the chief inspector.

"Two conductors. Three actors, three television personalities, two of Cooper's lads sitting together holding hands. No judge."

"That would be Judge Jophs, I presume," the chief said. He'd done his homework. Or rather, Keegan had done it for him.

"I've spoken with his house," I said, "and his housekeeper, or whoever was on the other end of the line, says he's here, in the Hall. We're looking for him."

The chief had raised the glasses to his eyes. I showed him where Harrigan was sitting, pointed out the bag on his lap. "That's Harrigan all right," the chief said. "I remember the photographs. He started early, playing with boxes of matches." He let the glasses hang on the cord round his neck. "Congratulations," he said, and I got the feeling he meant it.

"Now we'll go and face the superintendent."

"You're not going to clear the Hall?"

"Until the superintendent gets here, Inspector, it's your case. I'm just giving aid and assistance . . ."

"And keeping out of the line of fire . . . ?"

"That's one way of putting it."

Twenty cars were drawn up on the road that runs between the Park and the Hall. No moving traffic. So they'd already blocked the road. Without waiting for the chief superintendent. Already people were standing on the steps of the Memorial, gawping. They'd have a grandstand view, but be safe. I walked out until I could see two entrances. A policeman was standing near each one, looking uncomfortable. When the chief superintendent arrived about thirty seconds later he was wearing civilian clothing.

"Why haven't you cleared the Hall?" was the first thing he said to me as we went through the main door. The chief superintendent is small for a policeman, and can't weigh more than ten stones. He has that thin silvery hair that shows his scalp, which blushes when he's angry. Now it was bright pink. He turned and faced me. "Why hasn't the Hall been cleared?"

In for a penny, in for a pound. "Because I don't want the Hall cleared," I said, "and until someone relieves me of it, this incident is my responsibility. If you want to clear the Hall, sir, take over the incident." He didn't like that, but I'd judged well. The chief superintendent was a shouter. Shout first and ask questions later. Well, he damned well wasn't going to shout at me. I had too little to lose.

"Give me your reasons, man."

"With due respect, I'm an inspector, sir."

"Very well, Inspector, would you be so good as to state the reasons why you do not wish the Hall to be cleared."

That was better. I wasn't being awkward just for the sake of it, but I had to establish my status quickly if I was to get my points across. And with twenty cars outside, the roadway blocked, and doubtless evacuation having started from nearby premises, it was going to take all my arguing power to prevent them pulling rank on me.

"An anonymous note received. A known bomber sitting in the audience with a bag on his knee, a psycho, a nutter. He's threatened to kill the judge who sent him down. That judge is reported to be somewhere in the audience. It could be a knife, a gun, a bomb. I favour a bomb, because this man's a bomber. We can't clear the Hall without letting him know we're onto him. If we make any disturbance within that auditorium, if he sees ONE policeman, ONE action he can interpret as menacing, he could explode the device I believe he controls from inside that bag."

"Have you formed any opinion as to when he means to explode the bomb, assuming you to be right?"

"Yes. This work is choral as well as orchestral. The choral part is all in the last movement. I believe he means to wait until there's a choral crescendo, with the choir on its feet, before he pulls the detonator."

"And kills himself along with everybody else . . ."

"He's a psycho, sir, a nutter. I don't think he gives a damn."

"Have you located the judge? The one he threatened?"

"No sir, not yet."

He turned to the chief inspector. "What do you think, Chief?"

"He could be right, Chief Superintendent . . ."

"What are your plans?" the chief superintendent said to me.

"Find the judge. Try to get him out. Examine his immediate environment for any lethal device. If we find anything, pull Harrigan out as quietly as we can and try to get a cough . . ."

"And if you don't find the judge, or anything suspicious?"

"I deliberately haven't made a decision about that, Chief Superintendent. This whole matter must remain capable of review and change at a minute's notice. Whoever is in charge of the incident must be flexible. But above all, there must be no overt moves, no policemen in the Hall, no attempt to stop the concert . . ."

"I don't like it, Inspector."

That was better. Now he was prepared to discuss it with me.

"It's vitally important, sir, that the concert proceeds absolutely normally. Inside that concert hall must be an absolute oasis of silence, and peace. Out here, obviously, we must do everything possible to be prepared for whatever may happen . . ."

"In case you're wrong . . . ?"

"Or in case I'm right about police activity causing the nutter to explode his bomb, and you insist on filling the Hall with policemen, and stopping the concert . . ."

"Why shouldn't the chief inspector take over?"

"With respect, Chief Superintendent, I've been in and out of that box for the last thirty minutes, and Harrigan may have spotted me. Suspicious, but no more. After all I've been there for half an hour and nothing has happened, no signs of anyone stopping the concert. Every new face we introduce into that Hall increases the risk of Harrigan becoming suspicious . . ."

"I agree, Chief Superintendent," the chief inspector said. Good for him. At last, was I going to get his support? "But there is one thing I'd like to suggest . . ."

"Yes, Chief Inspector?"

"Clear the balcony and the upper circle . . ."

"It can't be done," I said, "without tipping off Harrigan."

"I did it in a cinema in Coventry. I don't see why it shouldn't work now. Incidentally, if we clear the balcony, at least we get out the students and I can interrogate them and remove them as a possible source of suspicion . . ."

"Look, Chief. You've been asking me all along to question the students, and so far I haven't done it. Okay, let's assume you've been right so far, and the students are responsible. Let's say they're harmless, that all they intend to do is chuck a few bags of flour on the stage, or spray a few soda syphons about. . . . You come into the balcony in force, and what happens? All the flour, all the soda water, go over that balcony in a hurry, plus maybe a few crackers to make a small bang. . . . And what happens then? You get a rush for the exits. Remember the football match? Remember the Criterion? How many deaths were caused by people just rushing for the exits?"

The chief inspector thought for a moment. So did the superintendent, but he wasn't going to be the first to speak. Very wisely. He'd come late into this; the chief inspector had been with it, though at one remove, all the time.

"We can't just do *nothing,*" the chief inspector said.

I shook my head. "We shouldn't do *anything* until we have a specific reason for doing it."

But he couldn't go along with that thinking. I could see it in his eyes. Okay, take a gamble. In my bones I felt the students were no longer involved, so the gamble was justified. Sloppy reasoning, I know, but I had to compromise somewhere, and my main objective was to keep them out of the lower part of that Hall. "Okay," I said, "get the students, and anybody else in that balcony, out. But for God's sake, Chief, no noise." It was an acceptable compromise. I sympathised with him. He had to do *something*.

"Work closely with Inspector Armstrong," the superintendent said, "but get as many people out as you can without arousing Harrigan's suspicions. Inspector, you concentrate on finding the judge and getting him out, and locating any bombs or other devices Harrigan may have planted. Use Cooper as a message between inside and out. I'll draw a cordon round the Hall and make preparations for any eventuality. I've already nominated this as a potential disaster area."

The chief inspector and I went back inside the Royal Hall. It hadn't escaped my notice that, if this did become a disaster area, we would be in the centre of it.

CHAPTER 6

The chief inspector took six uniformed constables up into the gallery and each walked down an aisle and placed himself against the railing, with his back to the orchestra out of sight of anyone in the bottom of the auditorium. The audience watched the arrival, but the brief murmur of comment rapidly died away when the constables did nothing.

Meanwhile, twelve other uniformed and helmeted constables had printed, with large letters on a foolscap sheet of paper, the following message.

THIS IS A POLICE MESSAGE. IT IS NOT A HOAX. WHEN YOU HAVE READ THIS PLEASE HAND IT TO THE PERSON SITTING NEXT TO YOU. THEN GET UP, QUIETLY, HOLDING THE SEAT SO THAT IT WILL NOT BANG, AND LEAVE THE HALL QUIETLY. A POLICE OFFICER OUTSIDE THE HALL WILL EXPLAIN: THIS IS NOT A HOAX. PLEASE LEAVE THE HALL AT ONCE, BUT IN ABSOLUTE SILENCE.

Six policemen started at the bottom of the aisles, and six halfway up, handing the note to the man sitting on the aisle. The silent exodus began. It had worked in Coventry, the chief inspector said; there was no reason it shouldn't work here. But, nevertheless, a part of him prayed. The Londoner is more sophisticated than the Midlander, less gullible and more suspicious. One or two people read the note, passed it along without doing anything about it; but when they saw other people getting up to leave, they followed. One man passed on the note without reading it. Nobody was going to sell him anything. The man next to him read the note, looked anxiously about him, gave it back to the first man, pointing to the text. The first man read it, got up, and scuttled out like a rabbit.

The chief inspector at the back of the Hall watched them leave, ready to wave his men in quickly should anyone object. No one did. One seat clanged when its owner tipped it back too quickly, but the sound was lost in the tumult from the orchestra and certainly could not have been heard below.

In five minutes the gallery was empty.

The police searched it, just in case, looking under every seat. They found nothing other than three umbrellas that had been forgotten, and two odd gloves.

Going down the back stairs, everyone with a briefcase was searched. Again, the police found nothing.

When I returned to the box I saw the booklet James Barrett had been holding, the list of patrons he knew by heart. Catch him missing an opportunity of greeting someone by name. I picked up the booklet. Cooper was watching me. "Eyes on Harrigan," I said. "I'm no oil painting." Sergeant Bates was still searching the Hall for the judge. I ran a finger down the list of patrons. The pearl in an oyster, a hard capsule of fact among the flesh of speculation?

J. P. Ormerod Braithwaite. Familiar name; a judge. Judges don't buy tickets for events; they either have tickets presented to them, *or* are patrons. I could hear the conversation as if in some inner ear. "Wouldn't mind hearing that chap Flughafer conduct the Beethoven, Ormerod Braithwaite . . ." Or are judges on first-name terms with each other?

"Really, Jophs. Why don't you avail yourself of my box . . . ?"

"Very civil of you . . ."

J. P. Ormerod's box was 22F.

I ran as silently as possible round the circular passageway behind the boxes. 22. C, D, E, the F. I opened the door only as far as was necessary to squeeze in. A curtain over the inside of the door had been drawn. I opened the curtain a crack and looked through. One person sitting in the box. Towards the back. A film star would have been hanging out of the front of the box like a starlet's breasts. The judge could see and hear, but not be seen. Thank God for that. His eyes were closed, but he was not asleep. Nor was he already dead. He must have sensed my presence, or perhaps opening the curtain had let in a draught, for he turned and looked at the slit in the curtain, a glint of annoyance in his eyes at being disturbed.

It was Judge Jophs, not Ormerod Braithwaite.

I had been right. Judges don't ring up and order tickets. They don't sit in seats with the hoi-polloi. They keep themselves remote from ordinary people, lead a solitary life in chambers, in courts, and in secluded boxes, private, untouchable. Until someone plants a bomb under them.

"My name is Inspector Armstrong, Judge. Please listen to me without speaking. Stay sitting down, Judge, and don't turn your head. Nod if you can hear and understand me," I whispered.

He had turned his head back towards the orchestra when I spoke, and now he nodded. I told him about the anonymous note and about Harrigan, sitting in the auditorium below. While I talked I searched the back of the box, running my hands over its surfaces. Lots of dust, but nothing that resembled an explosive device. No wires, no strings. Nothing beneath his chair, or the rail of the box. Nothing on the ceiling, though I daren't climb to examine it carefully. Nothing in the pockets of his overcoat except a pair of gloves. Nothing in his umbrella, nor in his hat. It need not be a bomb. It could be a needle in his hat band, poison dusted into his gloves. I reached up and took out the lightbulb, but its lack of weight told me nothing was hidden in there. Some villains are so clever they can take a lightbulb apart, fill it with heat-sensitive explosive and put it together again so the filament works. When you switch on, the heat activates the detonator and the bulb explodes, killing anyone the light shines on. When I'd assured myself there was nothing lethal in the box I crawled to the back and stood up out of sight.

"I'm still waiting for you to tell me what to do," the judge whispered. He wouldn't be used to that in his profession.

"Edge your chair back so you're completely out of sight."

He did as I asked, slowly, silently.

"Now, sir, perfectly naturally, come out of the box."

He was a tall man. When he stood at the back of the box and I was looking past his head, I saw the microphone. Or rather, I re-saw it. I'd noticed it when I was searching but had taken it for granted.

Now I looked at it through fresh eyes, remembering. "Someone's disconnected microphone four." This microphone was brown, in a box four by two by eight inches long, tapering to the bottom. It was hanging from the lower lip of the box above, tilted so that the flat face looked at the point in air where the judge's head had been. When sound waves strike the ribbon of a microphone, they make that ribbon vibrate inside a magnetic field. That vibration causes an electric current. In an acoustic detonator, it's possible to set the mechanism so that the bomb will explode only when the sound reaches a certain volume. Like a *molto fortissimo* passage in a work scored for full orchestra and choir . . . Like the passage near the end of the last movement of the Beethoven Ninth Symphony they were now playing.

A bomb, planted by Harrigan, in the microphone in the box.

"Perhaps you'll be good enough to tell me what this is all about," the judge said. I'd forgotten him.

"I'm sorry, sir, no time at the moment. Make your way down to the manager's office, and wait for me. I shall only be a few minutes and then I'll give you a complete explanation. . . ."

I raced down to the front door, beckoned to Keegan. "I want the Army. Fast but quiet. In Box 22F."

I ran to the BBC box, rang the telephone on the desk. The studio manager came on the line instantly.

"A microphone in Box 22F. Know anything about it?"

"Yes. There's one in each box along that row. We use them as extra commentators' mikes when we're doing a broadcast into Eurovision. The foreign-speaking announcers from Bush House sit in the boxes."

"How can the microphone be removed?"

"Dead simple. It's hanging on two spring-loaded brackets. Two hooks. Just unhook 'em. And then you'd need to separate the cable if it was still connected. Untwist the knurled ring, and then pull 'em apart."

"Thanks," I said.

Out of the box, along the corridor, running fast but silent.

The Army had not arrived when I got back to the box. "Where the hell are they?" I said to myself.

The microphone was hanging there. It looked innocent; any inanimate object hanging there would look perfectly innocent. Whoever bothers to look at a microphone these days, in a public place. Come to that, whoever even bothers to wave to the TV cameras anymore. Both have become commonplace, cameras and microphones. And 1984 will be here before we realise it. Damn it, where was the Army.

I moved the judge's chair slowly forward, to the side of the box. I stood on the chair, hidden by the curtain that hung down the side of the box from anyone in the audience. Only the orchestra and the choir could see me, and they were too busy with the music to bother about me. I reached out my arm. Along the underside of the pelmet. If the commentators used these microphones, there must be some way they could be brought lower down. That suspension would be flexible, somehow. I could reach the nearest part of it with the tips of my fingers. I gripped the suspension tightly, and slowly started to draw the microphone towards me. My God, don't let it jar.

The cords that suspended the microphone must have connected with counterweights. I could bring the microphone along under the pelmet, out of sight of the audience. I dare not glance down, round the curtain, to see if Harrigan was looking this way. I saw a couple of members of the waiting choir glance in my direction, and knew they had seen me, but choir discipline was good and they didn't whisper to each other or point at me. It couldn't be an acoustic detonator, it couldn't be an electrically operated detonator; and now I had the microphone about a foot from my face and I saw the cable was not connected to it, but twisted round one of the suspension cords. No connection went into the microphone, none I could see.

Gently, I unhooked the cord on the far side of the microphone, and passed the hook round the near cord before letting it go. I didn't want it to snap back and clatter across the box. No connections to the microphone; the bomb must be inside it and self-contained, with the detonator with it and a timing device. If that orchestra had not been blasting so loud, perhaps I'd have heard the tick of that timing device. Mostly they're clockwork, since that's the most reliable mechanism, though they can be a capsule of acid, with a slowly dissolvable plug. One thing was sure, *if* the microphone contained explosive it would also contain a detonator and a timing device, set to go off at the end of the Choral Symphony. It *must* be. Now I was holding the near cord in my left hand, and the microphone itself in my right hand, and slowly I slipped the cord hook out of the hole on the microphone's shank. I had to twist the cord to get the hook out, but it came without further difficulty. Sometimes, these detonators are sensitive to temperature, the heat of a sweating hand for instance. I clasped the microphone in my hand, and slowly drew it towards me, keeping it hidden behind the pelmet. My hand was sweating, but it felt cold. I felt cold, despite the warmth of that box. I could hear the microphone rustle along the inside of the pelmet; what sounded as a rustle would be a tempest to that ribbon inside, the one that generates the current. If I was wrong, if the explosive carried an acoustic detonator, this could be the end of all my troubles. No more Susan, and Sarah would get my commendation and pension. No more superintendent; no chief inspector; no Constable Cooper or Maurice Brigham. Just a complete nothing in small pieces. My heart was thumping, my eyes wet with sweat. Or tears? I lowered the microphone to my shoulder for safety, then slowly backed down and stepped off the chair, holding my body rigid. I walked backwards towards the door of the box, six inches at a time.

I gauged myself to be near the door, and almost dropped the microphone, when a voice said in my ear, "It's all right, Inspector, I have it now," and the weight of the microphone was lifted from my shoulder. I daren't grab at it to keep it there. I turned slowly. An Army major was standing in the doorway and at his feet was a box, with a spring-loaded contraption set in the centre of it. He was lowering the microphone into the contraption. Then he covered the microphone with a layer of cotton wool, and gently shut the lid. He grasped the handles, one each side of the box, picked it up gingerly, and proceeded to carry it.

I walked slowly beside him.

"Can you tell me anything about it, Inspector?" he asked.

"I think there is explosive inside it."

"Any idea what the explosive was meant for? To kill someone, to blow down a wall?"

"To kill someone."

"Ah, yes, I see." He was maddeningly calm. I could feel my heart thumping. "By the way, Inspector," he said, "you took a chance, bringing the microphone down from its suspension that way. I wish you'd waited for us."

"I wish you'd got here sooner," I said as I followed him.

"We went to the wrong box."

His sergeant was waiting down the corridor. Wearing headphones. Until that moment I hadn't realised the major was wearing a hearing aid, and what I took to be a throat microphone strapped round his neck. One man goes in to do the job. The other stays out of range at first. The first man talks while he's doing the job, and the second one listens. That way, if the bomb goes off only one man is killed, and the second man usually knows what he did wrong. For future reference.

I stood against the wall of the corridor, my knees trembling. I knew I had to sit down.

"Put your head between your knees, sir," the Army sergeant said. "It takes us that way sometimes, and we're at it all the time."

Cooper came along the corridor, looked hard at me, watched them carry away the box. I couldn't do that job for a million, cash in advance. Head between my knees, start to count slowly.

"You all right, Inspector?"

"I will be, in a minute."

"There's a phone call for you . . ."

"Take a message."

"I tried to, but she wouldn't give one. Insisted on speaking to you . . ."

"She . . ."

"She said, tell him it's Susan. . . ."

I hurried along the corridor to the telephone.

"Where are you, what are you doing? What the hell's going on?"

"I wanted to talk to you, but I couldn't get hold of you."

"Look, I can't talk now. I'll meet you at the Wimpy, later tonight, okay. Go there and wait for me."

She was crying at the other end of the telephone.

"Look, I can't stop now, Susan. Wait for me at the Wimpy."

"I've let you down," she said through her sobs. "I've let you down."

"Tell me about it at the Wimpy."

"I can't. I can't face you," she said, "not ever again."

Bloody girl. Histrionics at a time like this. Behaving like a kid of twelve. Let me down. What the hell did it matter.

"Snap out of it, Susan, and I'll see you later."

I'd taken the instrument away from my ear and was in the act of putting it back on its cradle when I heard her voice, faint, continuing to speak. *What was it she said?*

"No, it's too late, I'm going to kill myself."

And by the time I got the receiver back to my ear she'd gone. She hadn't hung the telephone on its cradle, just left it hanging there, I heard it knock against the side of the kiosk or wherever she was phoning from.

I ran down to the front hall.

"Look, Chief Inspector, I know you'll think I'm crazy, but somewhere in London there's a girl, and I think she's going to kill herself." Could I say that to him? On the strength of a half-heard sentence on a telephone from a girl who was emotionally immature. From a girl I'd unlawfully shielded from a charge of selling reefers?

He came across the Hall to me. "We've cleared the gallery," he said. "Have you made any progress?"

First things first. I couldn't tell him about Susan. Not then.

"Yes. I've found the judge, and I think I've found the bomb."

He looked in my face, doubtless seeing it white, strained, but not knowing all the reasons.

"Where's the bomb?"

"The Army has it. . . ."

His sigh of relief was almost as loud as the sound of the orchestra. "Well done, lad," he said, grabbing my arm. "bloody well done . . ."

"I'm not *sure,* Chief. I found a microphone. It had been disconnected apparently without reason. I checked with the BBC. The microphone was hanging over the judge's head."

"And now the Army has it . . . ?"

"Yes. They've taken it outside."

"They'll go into the Park I suppose?"

"Yes . . ."

"So we'll know soon enough. I was going to clear the next level. The upper circle. What do you think?"

"Your method worked in the gallery. I should try it again, Chief."

"What are you going to do?"

"Think, that's all I can do, for the moment."

But think about what? Harrigan, or Susan?

Harrigan first. *If* he's up to his old tricks, *if* he's nursed a grievance against the judge all these years. Damned irrational. But people are irrational. Look at Susan. She said she'd let me down. Okay, so some medical student had stuck his hand inside her pants and she'd liked it and let him. Harrigan could have stolen the microphone, taken it home and doctored it. . . . If only Susan had been to a decent girls' school, she would have developed normally, wouldn't have become so dependent on me that she'd feel badly about "letting me down." Hell, I couldn't spare the time to think about one silly girl when the lives of so many people in the Hall were at stake. Harrigan could have obtained the explosive; we're so lax in this country, as any doctor will tell you in any casualty ward on Guy Fawkes Day.

It had to be a time bomb. The Army would defuse it.

I could go into the Hall and pick up Harrigan, any time I wanted. Could I? What if the bomb wasn't in the microphone? Then all my former reluctance to stop the concert would become relevant again.

So, wait until you hear from the Army. Should only take minutes.

Susan? Forget about her. She'll be at the Wimpy later, with that look on her face.

I started to walk down to Barrett's office, but my legs were trembling so much I had to stop and lean against the wall. I looked at my hands. They were still trembling. You've got to let go sometime, haven't you? You can't go on bottling it up. You pick what you believe to be a live bomb off a ceiling that you believe could explode at any moment and blow your face to kingdom come. It doesn't matter that the bomb may be a figment of your imagination; at the moment you pick it off the end of the wire, you believe it to be real. You do it anyway. That's what you joined to do. We're all volunteers. We're all in it for what we can get out of it. Men still join the police force to try to get regular meals for their kids. Nobody does it for the money. Some do it for power, uniform, and the chance to strut down a street feeling like God Almighty. But even that goes when you become a detective and you have no visible source of authority. Most people think we do it because we're pigs, sadists. Some of us are. I don't think I am. I think I do it because it offers me my only chance to straighten people out, and preserve some sort of code of conduct. If I were dishonest enough I'd become a politician. When it all boils down, I suppose I'm a copper because I'm not qualified or intelligent enough to be anything else. It's a mug's game, a dog's life.

But by God, sometimes you feel like letting yourself go.

The last time I let myself go it cost me God knows how much seniority and promotion. I was out in a radio car, coming back from a punch-up in a pub; girls fighting like alley cats to protect the pimps who probably beat 'em every night of the week. I hadn't wanted to go back to the station. My duty time was up anyway but rather than go home I was riding round in the car, chatting with the lads, just like the old days. We were driving down Ken High Street when suddenly I saw this bag snatch. Young lad appeared to be waiting at the bus stop, fat old bitch walking along in a fur coat that must have cost a thousand. She had a bag as big as Gladstone's hanging on her arm, waving for a taxi. The boy was cute. He let her get halfway into the taxi, him holding the door open polite as could be, then he gave her a kick right up the arse that sent her sprawling on the rubber mat, fur coat an' all. Of course, when she felt the pain of the kick and started to fall forward on her face, she let go the bag, and he snatched it and ran. By that time we had stopped the car and I was out and running after him, like the good old days. All these pictures you see when the honest citizens run after a thief shouting "Stop" you can forget. The only man running after that lad was me; everybody else was busy getting out of the way, and I was too full of forty a day to do any shouting. This lad made his mistake. They all do. He ducked into an alley. I knew it was a cul-de-sac. I slowed down and went in on tip-toes. He was waiting for me, with a horn-handled knife you can buy in any Army Surplus Stores for picking your teeth. I got hold of the blade by mistake and it sliced my palm open, but I held onto it and then chopped him to the ground. When we got him to the car he tried it again. A woman standing nearby grabbed my shoulder. "Leave that poor lad alone," she screeched. "He's got blood all over him. . . ."

It was *my* blood. While the woman distracted my attention, he kneed me in the balls. But I let him have it. I can remember exactly what I was thinking. That bloody woman, blood all over my only good suit, and detectives don't get a uniform allowance, and now he's kneed me in the balls. The first hit smashed his front teeth and the second broke his jaw. From that day on they nicknamed me "Thumper" in the division, and though the official court of inquiry cleared me and lifted my suspension, it took a long while for the nickname to be forgotten. These trembling hands earned me that nickname. I shoved them in my pocket and walked down the corridor.

The judge was waiting with James Barrett. Barrett had a glass of sherry in front of him. The judge was standing stock still, waiting. No glass of sherry would be strong enough for him at that moment.

"Why haven't you cleared the Hall, Inspector?" he asked.

His voice would have cut a steel bar.

"Don't you understand, man, that four thousand people are in danger here. And why isn't the chief superintendent taking charge . . . ?" An inspector didn't count, eh? Nothing less than a chief superintendent for his honour the judge.

"I have only a few questions for you, sir, and you would oblige me by answering them quickly. We certainly don't have any time to waste on fruitless speculations. . . ." That got to him. Men's lips do tighten when they are angry, and become lighter in colour. His did.

"Have you had any contact with, or received any messages from, a man named Mike Harrigan since you sentenced him to fifteen years approximately ten years ago?"

"None whatsoever . . ." Good. I'd made him angry enough to cooperate with me. Later, of course, he'd try to pick off my skin in small pieces for the benefit of the commissioner, but I had no time to think about what would happen later.

"Have you received any anonymous notes, any threatening letters, any communications of any kind that would cause you to believe an attempt might be made on your life?"

"None whatsoever . . ."

"Was your decision to attend this concert a planned matter, or did you decide at the last minute?"

"I arranged it with the owner of the box as soon as I heard they had abandoned the pop concert and were intending to substitute the Beethoven . . ."

"Almost a month ago?"

"Yes."

"Have you any idea how many people might have known you were coming to the concert tonight?"

"I don't know how many people watch television. You apparently don't. Anyone who was watching three weeks ago could have known. I was taking part in a discussion programme. There was a suggestion that the judiciary do not involve themselves in the affairs of the day and are out of touch. I stated this was not so and quoted several of my own extra-judiciary interests, including my love of classical music and my intention of attending this concert . . ."

Bingo. Harrigan had been watching the TV. Saw a familiar face, heard the judge say he would attend this concert, and started his planning. How he had known the judge would be at this concert had been a major stumbling block; but of course Harrigan could have watched TV. Nutters think cool and calm sometimes, often make most careful plans for a bout of lunacy. And why shouldn't he follow the same process of deduction I'd followed to find the judge? Or rather, to find out where the judge was going to sit. . . . Ormerod Braithwaite's name was on the list of patrons, and there is nothing secret about that document. One telephone call: "This is the booking office of the Royal Hall speaking, Mr. Ormerod Braithwaite. Do you intend to occupy your box on the night of the concert since we'd like to take the carpet up for cleaning . . ."

"Have you finished, Inspector," Mr. Justice Jophs asked me, "or do you propose to continue to interrogate me?"

I had time for a little private public relations work. "I'm sorry to impose my questions on you, sir, and wouldn't do so if, in the course of my duty, I didn't believe them to be necessary. Already you've been of the most tremendous help to me, and I'm certain the superintendent will agree with me about that. One last request, sir. Please don't go back into that Hall. Not just yet. If you do so, I believe you may be in danger."

"I presume that at some time you will inform me as to what that danger might be . . . ? Though I can make my own guess."

"A full explanation will be forthcoming sir, either from me or from the superintendent. And now, if you will excuse me . . ." I know he would have preferred me to back out, bowing, but I turned and ran.

Take a chance. The bomb's in the microphone. So get Harrigan out of there. Two of us. But first, a quick phone call. "Arthur, I think that girl may be back at the hostel. Could your girl check again?"

"Anything wrong?"

"I don't know, I honestly don't know."

"Let me put it this way. Shall we check the bathrooms?"

Where else would you go to kill yourself?

"Yes."

"Like that, is it?"

"I don't know."

"Can I ask you a personal question? Not involved, are you? I have a job to keep."

"Arthur, I am personally involved, but not that way."

"And you want it kept quiet . . . ?"

"If you can without any problems . . ."

"I'll try my best."

"Thanks, Arthur." I put the phone down.

Two of us would do the snatch. Sergeant Bates and I. Skelton standing by unidentified to run interference if necessary. Slow in, but quick out. Smother your man, grab him, out. No fuss. We do a lot of it nowadays, but you have to be careful.

Once I caught my hand in the waistband of a pair of trousers, and when we lifted I ripped her trousers and pants off her. Accident, of course, but I expect you saw the pictures. Two years ago even the Sundays would have retouched the pics to hide what she was showing.

Sergeant Bates and me. I briefed him as we walked along the circular corridor at the back of the Hall. He was hard and cold, imperturbable. I might have been telling him we were going to pick daisies. Into the Hall at the back. Down the aisle, slowly but purposefully. The trick is to look as if you're going somewhere but nowhere important. Like you've just remembered the ashtrays need emptying. My favourite dodge is to count heads, making it obvious. Then they think you're from market research. These days anybody can go up to anybody and say, "We're conducting a survey," and the gullible general public will tell them anything. We've even got a class of sex-offenders. Go up to young girls in the street. Get the girls to tell them how many times they've had it and with whom. Don't think about Harrigan. Not yet. Thoughts can communicate themselves. We caught a man once. A pervert. Going round the suburbs. Couldn't believe it, just couldn't. "I'm conducting a survey on behalf of the Home Office. What sizes of clothing would be required in the case of an atomic war. It's skin-tight radiation-shielding plastic. I'll have to measure you, madam, without your clothes." Think I'm joking? Fifty-six women fell for it and let him loose with his tape, standing, sitting, lying starkers on a bed. Fifty-six before one woman complained to her husband. I counted heads. One fellow looked annoyed but said nothing. A woman told her husband, his head bowed no doubt in bored sleep, to lift his head up so's not to be missed out.

But all the time I was watching the back of Harrigan's head.

Skelton had noticed us. A copper's sixth sense. I knew what he'd be feeling. No overt movements, no heavy breathing, no feet shifts to ease cramped muscles. Suddenly, your stomach rumbles. Sounds like Vesuvius. Dammit, why not. Usually you've been on duty for a solid thirty-six hours and all you've eaten in that time is a corned beef sandwich with a dash of Harold's Pride on it, cups of tea with lots of sugar to give you instant energy, or so they say, your guts swilling with bile. Skelton would guess what we intended; we could rely on him to get the black bag. Above all I didn't want to have to say "Watch that man, he's got a bomb in his bag." Panic waves spread faster than forced wedding gossip and bomb is a word which causes instant reaction.

Ten yards to go. Sergeant Bates pulled his hand down to clear his wrists from his cuffs to give him easier movement. "Steady," I thought, "keep your movements to a minimum. Little things give you away." I knew Sergeant Bates would be nervous, but so was I. So would Skelton be. This was "over the top," without a rifle.

You do a thing you've done successfully a hundred times

before, but the instant before you do it, just after the point of no return, the thought comes quickly into your mind that this will be the one time it doesn't work, the one time an unpredictable and therefore incalculable something will happen. Such stupid things. Slipping on a carpet, sliding on a patch of oil on a pavement. Uncontrollable coughing, or sneezing. You're a human being, and putting on the blue doesn't entitle you to any divine protection. Rain falls equally on the just and the unjust. And though you're the hunter and take the initiative, you have none of the thrill of the chase, the extra adrenaline of the exhilaration of "the sport." You're human, your stomach ties itself in knots and you want to piss. Sometimes you do. You walk slowly across a room at night and know someone is hiding in the deep dark. You know he holds a gun in his hand and sweeps a tight arc as he listens for any sound of movement, any whisper you might make. The gun's loaded. Every nerve end in your body jangles, spittle in your mouth you daren't swallow because even a swallow is loud in a silence. You're afraid but drawn forward by the fear since to prolong it would be worse. You're desperate as he is, but your desperation is often compounded of trivia. "Don't let me catch it tonight; I'm coming up for pension/promotion/leave next week. Let's get it over with" thuds through your mind like a diesel engine. You have no desire for heroics, no "will to right the wrongs of the world," no wish to die. You know how to walk without making a noise—toe first and then the rest of your foot down; it makes your ankles ache but it's worth it. You keep your legs apart and your arms in front of you with your hands touching lightly, and hear the rustle of the cheap coarse serge suit you wear because you can afford nothing better on a policeman's pay, but you know the chances are that he's wearing a flashy silk or a mohair and they rustle like crinkled silver foil, and that's a consolation. You ease your way forward into that impenetrable blackness trying not to feel sorry for yourself. And not succeeding.

Only two paces to go. Bates to the left, counting. Stop. Stand still, eyes along the rows, overtly counting. No movement from Harrigan, no interest; he's listening to the music. . . .

End of the row. Look at Skelton. He looks back. Small jerk with your head, upwards and away. He gets the message. Bloody radar, isn't it? Or ESP. People are looking at you. Can't avoid that. Nudge Sergeant Bates and look at Skelton again. The people looking at you switch and look at Skelton. Bend forward and whisper to the man at the end of the row, "Excuse me, please." He gets up, doesn't bother to look along the row, assumes you must have seen empty seats. Skelton gets up, says to the man on his right, "Excuse me, please." The man on his right gets up. Now everybody thinks one man is going out, and two men are coming in. It's a puzzler for the people who can see all along the row and know there aren't two spare seats, but they do nothing about it. You ease in. The second man gets up without being asked. The third man, bloody uncivil bastard, won't get up but turns his knee, making you scrape past him. All right, lad, you'll suffer on the way out. Now Skelton's standing in front of the man on the next seat to him, and appears to be having difficulty getting past. Sergeant Bates is coming along the row behind you. So far it's only taken a fraction of a second but it seems like an eternity. You see Harrigan's head turn round, or rather start to turn round, to look at Skelton, who's practically leaning over him, and then as Harrigan's head starts to turn the other way, you pounce. A snatch. A straight snatch and lift, just like they do with the bar bells. Harrigan's leaned slightly forward to avoid Skelton and that's taken his back off the seat. You reach round him and past him and your hand goes under his right armpit. Sergeant Bates reaches past you and his hand goes under Harrigan's left armpit, and you grunt "hup" and the two of you lift Harrigan straight up over the back of his seat and drag him along the row you've just come through. And there's a helluva confusion. The man who wouldn't stand up when you came in gets the side of his head clouted by Harrigan's heel, but you heave and push your way backwards, sensing the start of the crowd reaction and the noise of people saying "What the hell's happening?" and the man with the clouted ear protesting, and then Harrigan's clear in the aisle and his feet drop to the ground and now that he has a purchase this could be the moment he regains his balance and starts to run but you chop behind his knees, let go his shoulders, and he goes backwards, flat on his back, with a bang that knocks all the wind from his body. Before he can breathe again Sergeant Bates grabs his hands and you grab his feet and rush him up the aisle and out of the Hall. Skelton follows, with Harrigan's bag, saying, "I think he was a sex pervert, a sex pervert," and that's the one thing anybody will believe of anybody, even the most respectable-looking men, and not wish to interfere.

The orchestra didn't play a wrong note, didn't miss a single beat. In the corridor we flipped Harrigan over so his face was towards the floor and ran him along the corridor of the manager's office. Skelton passed us and held the door open and we dropped Harrigan on his face on the carpet. In front of the judge, and James Barrett.

I suddenly realised. Harrigan hadn't made a sound or a move. I flipped him over. He was out cold. "This, I suppose," the judge said, "is the man you called Harrigan?"

Soon the Army would open the microphone, find what Harrigan had hidden there, and telephone. Soon I'd have the evidence to ram in this bastard's teeth. "Yes, this is Harrigan," I said. Sergeant Bates emptied Harrigan's pockets. Handkerchief, tickets, letters. Packet of cough drops, another handkerchief, a leather wallet containing twenty-two pounds. Nothing else. No pens, no notes. What kind of a man would go on a job, running the risk of dying with two dirty handkerchiefs?

Skelton opened the bag gingerly. Just because we think there's something in the microphone, we can't ignore his bag. A box of chocolates, a pullover, with a darned sleeve. They teach 'em sewing and darning in prison. A pair of shoes that had just been cobbled. Full sole and heel. Costs a fortune these days. Wouldn't think he'd been out long enough to wear down a pair of shoes. Do they let them wear their own shoes in prison? I'd never thought about it. Do they get an issue of prison boots, or wear their own? And if so, what happens on a long sentence when the shoes wear out? A lot of the shoes you buy these days can't be repaired.

At the bottom of the bag was a small screwdriver such as electricians (and, I imagine, BBC microphone technicians) use, and a pair of side-cutting pliers. We'd never make a charge of "being in possession of house-breaking tools" on the strength of an electrician's screwdriver and pliers. Not that I had any thought of a holding charge; I was confident the Army would give me all the evidence I needed once they got that microphone open. A pocket knife; sharp but without a flick blade. A nick on the blade; that knife had been placed across live wires and a spark had chewed out that nick. A transistor radio in a leather case, just an ordinary transistor, not a radio controller, and that was the lot. Nothing else in the bag. No extra bomb for good measure.

The judge and James Barrett were talking quietly in the corner, the judge asking Barrett what this was all about. Barrett had no satisfactory replies. He looked as if he were standing in a witness box on a particularly nasty charge. I went across to them.

"Do you recognise this man, sir?" I asked.

He shook his head slowly, searching his memory. Harrigan was regaining consciousness. "He threatened to kill you, sir," I prompted. "I was in court at the time . . ."

"I hear many threats," the judge said, "I'm afraid I'm long past taking any of them seriously."

"Is everything all right now?" Barrett asked. "I mean, there's no more danger? We needn't clear the Hall?" I looked at him. This had passed him by, hadn't it.

"If it's all over, can't you take him to the police station?" Harrigan might have been garbage he wanted removing to the dump. "I can't see why you had to bring him in here, anyway. It's a criminal matter. The sooner you lock that man up the better. I'll have to give a full report to the board of trustees, you know. We shall have dreadful complaints, you carrying him about the Hall that way. . . ."

He wanted no more of Harrigan, no more of me, of us. People will call us in, stand behind while we take what risks are necessary, and then can't stand the sight of us when we've done it. They utter expressions of gratitude, talk a lot of crap like "you deserve a commendation," "I'll get to see the chief constable hears about this," and never even offer a cup of tea to calm our jangled nerves. They cannot take upon themselves the responsibility of what will happen to the criminal once we've caught him. They think of him sitting behind bars for the next few years and blame us for putting him there. Lots of 'em go so far as to refuse to identify a criminal at line-up. We know they know it's the man, but they can't bring themselves to put the finger on him to send him away. They hope we'll find some inanimate piece of evidence that will convict him without them taking any responsibility.

"I think I've found what might be a bomb," I said, "but others may have been planted. . . ." That wiped the smug frown off his face. I thought he was going to faint at the thought we might have to go through the whole routine again. "I'd be grateful if you'd sit in that box and keep an eye on things for me, since you know the routine at these concerts. . . ."

I thought he was going to have a fit.

"Me sit in a box, and *me* keep an eye on things. That's policeman's work . . ."

"And I've already got Constable Cooper doing it."

"Really. This is *too* much." He left the room in what can only be described as a flutter, the dancing motion of a butterfly. Not that I cared.

Harrigan was fully recovered. They'd dumped him on a chair. "You're Mike Harrigan, aren't you?"

"And you're the officer they call 'the Thumper.' "

Tit for tat. He'd recognised me; now he grinned.

"We have to have something to talk about on exercise," he said. Then he turned his head. "Good evening, Judge," he said.

The judge nodded his head.

"You know this officer," Harrigan said, to the judge. "He's the big bold detective who carries all the wrongs of the world on his broad shoulders. He has a reputation. He likes to thump people like me . . ."

"No one will thump you while I am here," the judge said.

We have a standard procedure in this country not many people know about outside the police force and the legal profession called "the Judge's Rules." It's explained for the average copper in Moriarty's Police Law, the young copper's bible. The Judge's Rules state not very precisely exactly what a policeman may and may not do when he confronts a suspect. Some say the Judge's Rules protect the criminal, but they're a pain in the neck when you're involved in the ruck-a-muck of a criminal investigation. They're always talking about changing them, but the changes never seem to operate in favour of the police, only to tie him in more and more red tape. Freedom of the individual. Civil rights. Judge's Rules—they make me sick. A copper's either bent or he isn't, he's either a nut case before he joins the force or he isn't. If only they'd spend a bit of money on medical and psychiatric investigation of coppers, if only they'd try to help a copper live through the dreadful stresses and strains, they wouldn't need Judge's Rules. I know a hundred coppers, and I know only one I'd like to call a pig. He'll never make sergeant. I'm not trying to whitewash the police force—I'm just trying to scrape away some of the dirt that gets thrown, to reveal us in our true colour. Which is just the same colour as any other decent human being. Judge's Rules are a lame-duck approach to a problem. Most criminals have no experience of the law, and though we may catch them, to be punished they have to be convicted *according to the law*. And the law is administered by solicitors, as venal, as dishonest, as ignorant, as lazy, as misinformed as the rest of humanity. You don't make a man more honest or more criminal by making him into a solicitor, or by making him into a copper. But coppers have to face the practicality, while solicitors dabble about with the theory. And the Judge's Rules are designed not to help maintain the law, but to benefit criminals and lawyers. And you can quote me.

Certainly a lot of criminals have gone scot-free because the police weren't allowed to bounce 'em around the wall a bit. "As soon as a police officer has evidence which would afford reasonable grounds for suspecting a person has committed an offence, he shall caution that person," the Rules say. It doesn't give you any help in translating those words into reality. What is EVIDENCE? Was that microphone EVIDENCE? Was that anonymous note EVIDENCE? Put together, did they give me reasonable grounds for suspecting? And did Harrigan's past history give me reasonable grounds for suspecting *him*.

I stood in front of Harrigan. He looked at me, cheeky.

"You've had your say; now I'll have mine . . ."

"This is where he starts thumping me, Judge," Harrigan said. "He's going to start asking me questions, and with each question he'll thump me, and when I've had enough of being thumped I'll agree to anything he cares to suggest, and he'll write it down as a statement, that'll be read out to you in court. . . ."

By God I could have thumped him, right then and there. The judge was looking at me. He knew what I had to do. I knew.

"Michael Harrigan. I am going to ask you some questions. You're not obliged to say anything unless you wish to do so . . ."

"But if I don't you'll thump me . . ."

"Would you please hold your tongue, Harrigan, for a moment . . ."

"So that you can caution me, in the official language . . . ? Why should I hold my tongue? Once you've cautioned me, you'll start thumping me. I don't like violence. I'm a coward. I can't stand any kind of brutality whether it comes from yobbos or the police. Hurt me and I'll say anything, I swear I will. You know that. But you'll thump me to make me talk quickly so you can boast back at the station you 'got a quick cough' out of me."

He had the cunning of a madman, but I'd never seen one so certain, so poised. Did the judge have a smile on his lips or was that his normal out-of-court expression. He knew damn well what I had to do under Judge's Rules; somehow I had to get out the official caution and use it on Harrigan, before he said much else.

". . . you are not obliged to say anything unless you wish to do so," I intoned, looking at neither Harrigan nor the judge, "but anything you *do* say *may* be put down in writing and given in evidence." Sergeant Bates had taken out his notepad and pencil. "This is the manager's office of the Royal Hall, Kensington," I said, "the date is the third of

March, the time is 2050 hours, ten minutes to nine, and present in this room with you is Mr. Justice Jophs, Sergeant Bates, Detective Constables Cooper and Skelton, and myself. Ah yes, and that is also being written down by Sergeant Bates."

It was all there, as prescribed in the Judge's Rules, but this was the first time I'd ever used them in the presence of a judge.

At first Harrigan was silent, looking at me, then at the judge. "It was my birthday yesterday," he finally said. "They clubbed together at the digs and bought me a walnut sponge, with chocolate icing. Wasn't that good of them?"

The judge was looking at me, shaking his head from side to side. Oh my God, I'd goofed again. There are two forms of caution. One you must use if you intend to charge the suspect with an offence. The one I'd used is only meant for those occasions when you haven't yet made up your mind whether to charge the suspect or not. The judge knew I'd made up my mind. Thank God Harrigan so far had said nothing about the crime. Harrigan knew, too. That was why he was looking at the judge, and prattling on about his birthday, hoping I hadn't noticed my mistake. Clever as a box load of monkeys . . .

But what would the charge be? Murder? Unlawfully and maliciously causing an explosion likely to endanger life? What would they charge him with? No explosion had occurred. No one had been murdered, or even injured, so I couldn't charge him with that. Section 2. How did it go? Unlawfully and maliciously doing any act with intent to cause an explosion, *whether such explosion takes place or not*. Thank God for the final clause, the rider. That would hold Harrigan. Whether the explosion takes place or not. Unlawfully and maliciously. We could get him for damage to property, to whit one BBC microphone. Maliciously?

Well, he'd threatened the judge in public and the court reporter was bound to have a note of that. Back at the station they could throw the book at Harrigan page by page. The superintendent would love that. One of his maxims, and he had many, was "always charge a man with EVERY offence you can find." Then if the suspect was found not guilty on one of the charges, you could always hope they'd catch him on one of the others.

The judge was becoming impatient.

"If you'd like to go back into the Hall to hear the rest of the symphony, sir . . ." I said.

"I will stay here, Inspector. Thank you," he replied. He wanted to hear me make a damned fool of myself by proceeding without the proper caution.

"Now then, Mr. Harrigan," I said, playing out the moment. "It is my intention to put some questions to you about a possible offence . . ." The word *possible* was mine, inserted into the official jargon at the last moment. I wouldn't know until I'd heard from the superintendent and he'd heard from the Army if any offence had taken place. "I repeat, I intend to put some questions to you about a possible offence for which you may be prosecuted . . ."

Now the judge was nodding approval and, the bit between my teeth, I cantered through the caution, the possible charges, the lot. Harrigan looked at me. At least I'd wiped that damned smirk off his face. "You going to thump me now?" he asked. This time, he meant it.

A judge was watching every move I made, and well over four thousand people were sitting within a few yards of us, and maybe their lives as well as my own were ticking away. I turned to look at the judge.

"I would like to interrogate this person alone, sir," I said. He wasn't falling for that one.

"With your permission, Inspector, I'll stay."

"The case we are involved in has a special nature."

"You'd be surprised how many people say that to me in court. Especially when they've done something they ought not to have done."

"We've received an anonymous note, sir, saying that at the end of this symphony someone will be dead. I suspect an explosion device has been planted in a microphone, and I shall know about that as soon as the proper authorities have completed their investigation."

"Then we'd better wait for that, hadn't we?"

"With respect, sir, I can't wait. I believe that any explosive device planted in the Hall was put there with the express intention of killing you, but the Hall is full of people who are not concerned with any motives of revenge this man may have had against your person, and it is my intention and my duty to protect those people."

"By interrogating this man . . . by thumping him?" I restrained my anger. I had a reputation for handling people.

"I intend to question this man. He has a history of association with explosive devices. I want to discover if he has planted an explosive device inside the Hall. And if so, where it is. This will necessarily be a brief interrogation, and any expedient I may employ to hasten his replies seems to me to be justifiable, in view of the danger to the great number of people in that Hall. . . ."

He was shaking his head. I'd been glancing at Harrigan's eyes. He had great self-control. No flicker to show he knew he was the man we were talking about. The judge wouldn't take it from me the polite way, I could see that. Then Harrigan smirked at me. That did it.

"Look, you," I said, angry. "I want to know what you've been up to. I want to know if there is a bomb in that Hall. And I intend to find out as quickly as possible."

Harrigan looked at the judge. "Let me advise you of your rights in this matter," the judge said, ignoring me. That's what did it.

"Sergeant Bates," I said, indicating the judge, "as your senior officer I order you to escort this man out of this room. If he refuses to go with you peacefully, I order you again to use such minimum force as is necessary to take him to the station where, in due course, I will charge him with obstructing a police officer in the execution of his duty."

"You'd arrest *me,* Inspector?" the judge said.

"At this moment, sir, I would do anything to get you out of here."

Sergeant Bates was a copper through and through, and he'd received a direct order from a superior officer. He walked across the room and stood before the judge, and when he spoke, his voice, unintentionally I'm sure, was a parody of the police voices you still hear on Saturday night television. "Now come along, sir, you heard the Inspector," he said soothingly, "come along peacefully with me and leave him sort out this bit of bother. . . ."

Bit of bother? Four thousand people possibly sitting on a bomb?

"Fetch your superintendent, Sergeant," the judge said, but Sergeant Bates shook his head. "The inspector's in charge here, sir." The judge realised he could do nothing to dissuade the sergeant from taking him out of the room, by "minimum" but effective force if necessary. Sergeant Bates was the type of policeman *no one* can intimidate.

"Harrigan," the judge said, "look at me."

Harrigan did so. The judge glanced quickly at me, then looked back at Harrigan, wearing his court-room expression. "I'm going to ask you one question, Mr. Harrigan, and I want a truthful answer. Have you planted a bomb this evening . . . ?"

Bloody fool, and him a judge. He'd asked three questions in one. Damn these bloody amateurs. Interrogation is a job for the specialists. He should have asked, "Is there any explosive device in or near the Hall?" But no, he'd asked three questions and a NO to any part of the question would get Harrigan off the hook. Have *you* planted a bomb this evening? Specimen answer, No, sir, and the truth would be that an accomplice had planted it. Question two. Have you planted a *bomb* this evening? Specimen answer, No, sir, and the truth could be that he'd planted a land-mine, not a bomb, and a land-mine by definition is not a bomb. And finally, question three, and this was the easiest to evade. Have you planted a bomb *this evening?* No, sir. Because he'd planted it this afternoon. I knew damned well he hadn't planted a bomb this evening. There hadn't been time. If he'd planted one, it would have been this afternoon when the orchestra was rehearsing and all sorts of odd bods were in the building, getting ready for the concert this evening.

"Come along, man, that's a simple question," the judge said with some asperity. But Harrigan knew, didn't he. He looked at me and almost smiled, and when he turned back to the judge he could have been saying, "You're not behind the bench now, cock!" But all he said out loud was "No, sir." No, sir, to which question? Not this evening, not a bomb, not him?

The judge turned to me. "I believe him," he said.

"You have your orders, Sergeant."

"Now come along, sir, come along. You're only making things more difficult for yourself."

"Before I go," the judge said, "let me give you a warning. I shall personally examine this man when you've finished with him, and if I find any signs of anything untoward . . ." And then my patience broke. Dammit, there was no time, no time. "You are resisting an officer in the course of his duty. Sergeant, for God's sake, get him out of here and don't let him say another word." His long upper lip quivered for a moment, but then he had the good sense to go. I wiped my hands down the seams of my trousers. He'd never know how close he'd come to the bum's rush. Skelton and Cooper were left in the room with Harrigan and me. "You two outside as well," I said. I knew Cooper'd take up a position at the door. "And you, Skelton, on the door, and nobody else within ten yards. We don't want Cooper getting earache. . . ."

They both went out. That left me. And Harrigan, sitting on a chair. I stood in front of him. He looked old but sprightly like a twinkling gnome. Prison ages a man they say. His jowls sag, features lose definition, skin turns to grey putty. Harrigan had avoided all that. His cheeks were pink with health, his merry eyes smiling at me. He was a nutter, a madman, but clean and neat and tidy. His fingernails had been looked after; he had a crease in his trousers, his clothes fitted him, his shirt had been laundered, and the knot of his tie was neat and tidy in the centre of his collar. No, he wouldn't care for human violence. His was the remote but cataclysmic eruption of explosives, the crackling tearing violence of shock waves and flames, ear-shattering, eardrum-beating noise and the orgiastic long slow rumble of complete destruction.

I hit him hard. Across that pink, washed, smiling face. With the back of my hand. That way it hurts him more, me less. He was starting to fall sideways off the chair and I hit him again on the other cheek and that brought him upright again. He didn't make a murmur, but I could tell he was shocked beyond words. In a sense, the judge had softened him up for me. He didn't believe I'd hit him with the judge's threat hanging over my head. Being unexpected the blow was more terrifying. A trickle of blood ran down his lip from his left nostril. The pain in his face must have been intense.

Both cheeks bore the marks of my fingers, the hard knuckles and hand bones, and tears flushed his eyes. Before he could lift his hand to wipe them away I hit him again, one each side, smashing my hand across his face with every bit of violence that was in me. He staggered on the chair, and I caught the sudden whiff of an old man's fear, and old man's sweat glands and bladder going out of control. Now the red blotches were forming again; as the blood came back, so more pain would come. He was an old man, and I was a strong young man, and I was beating him.

"Now you know that I'll thump you. . . ."

Fear in his eyes, and a glint of his madness, his hatred. If he survived this I'd be on his list with the judge, but I didn't care.

"Now you *know* I'll thump you. . . . But let me tell you why. I believe you have planted a bomb somewhere inside that Hall. It may be inside that microphone, in which case we've got it out of there, safe and sound. But it may not be in that microphone. It may be somewhere else. You're a bomber, Harrigan, and you're a nut, and reasoning is no good against men like you. But this is something you will understand. I'm going to thump you until I'm satisfied there's no bomb hidden in the Hall. Do you understand that? I'm going to *thump* you until *I am satisfied* there's no bomb in the Hall. And what you must work out for yourself is, how much thumping you can stand, how much pain you can stand, before you tell me what I want to know."

"You wouldn't thump me if the judge was here," he said.

"That's why I sent him away," I said. I hit Harrigan again. One, two, three, four, each one across his cheeks. Now the blood was pouring out of each nostril, his tie knot was no longer in the centre of his collar, the stain of his piss was spreading over his trousers and he stank abominably of sweat and fear. "Is there a bomb in the Hall?" I asked him each time I hit him with my left hand, and each time I hit him with the right I asked, "Did you plant a bomb in the microphone?"

I hated myself for what I was doing. I knew the judge would have me for this, and the chief inspector and the superintendent. It's madness to interrogate a suspect when you're the only police officer in the room. The chief inspector should be there, and a uniformed constable, or a sergeant. Harrigan would have me for this and any court in the country would convict. I believed there was a bomb in that Hall, the lives of over four thousand people were in danger, and there was no time for finesse. Harrigan was a madman. I had only one hope of getting through to him, and that through his hatred of personal violence.

The orchestra had started the last movement, but I found it hard to concentrate on them sufficiently to estimate where they were. The choir was singing but I couldn't say how long that movement had been on. The silence between Harrigan and myself, however, was as tangible as an unplucked violin string and just as taut. I hit him again.

I reckoned I had two hits left before the pain anaesthetised itself, before he ceased to feel the blows when I hit him.

He laughed. I could see the movement was painful to him, but he managed it just the same.

"What do you want me to say? Yes? No?"

"Is your name Harrigan?"

"Yes."

"Have you just come out of prison?"

"Eight months ago . . ."

"Why were you in prison?"

"Because I planted a bomb in a girls' school."

"Have you planted a bomb in the Royal Hall?"

"What do you want me to say, yes, or no?"

I hit him again. Only one hit left. But, dammit, only a few minutes left of that Beethoven symphony. Now I could make out the words the choir were singing: "All mankind are brothers plighted where thy gentle wings abide . . ."

"Why did you put the bomb in the girls' school . . . ?"

"Funny thing, you're the first copper ever asked me that. Throughout the trial nobody asked me *why*. They assumed I was daft, and that was it. . . ." Now he was laughing again, and I could see he was waiting for me to thump him again. Willing me to hit him again. Never hit a man when he wants it. Never let a man anticipate it, prepare himself against it. "I put it there because I objected to the school's religious education policy. I don't believe in teaching young kids about hell."

Keep him talking. Get him into the habit of answering questions. Then give him the one you're interested in.

"Why use a bomb? Why not shoot the Religious Knowledge teacher?"

"I liked bombs in those days . . ."

"That's why you used a bomb tonight . . . ?"

"Have I used a bomb tonight?"

Quick, wipe that one out, but save that last hand hit. Don't use it now, don't waste it. "Why did you come tonight?"

"I like music. Especially classical. There's so much pop about." Holy Jesus Christ and Mary, there's a bloody bomb in there and here we are talking about pop music.

"Who gave you the ticket?"

"A man at the Labour Exchange. . . . How did you know somebody gave it to me . . . ?"

"Instinct . . ." Try humour. "I'm not just a pretty face . . ."

"*I* won't be, either, when *you've* finished with me. . . ."

Strange how it happens. Start an interrogation with a couple of smacks across the face and before you know what's happening you're chatting like two old mates. . . .

"When did they give you the ticket. Yesterday? Week ago . . . ?"

"No, at least a month ago." That was good. I had him

going so well he was interrupting me. But we still needed to hurry. The last movement of the Beethoven lasts just over twenty-five minutes. The orchestra starts first, plays for eight minutes before the chorus begins. And the chorus was now singing—"Ye to whom the boon is measured, friend to be of faithful friend . . ." twenty-five minutes take away ten. Oh my God. And all I'd established was one fact, that he'd known about the concert, he'd had his ticket long enough to have made plans about it.

"So you've had the ticket a month . . . ?"

"I didn't say that. I knew about it a month ago. I didn't know at the time it was a pop concert. Royal Hall. I thought it would be something classical. But when I read it was a pop concert, I didn't bother to pick up the ticket . . ."

"But you changed your mind when you read they'd substituted Beethoven?" Or more likely, when he'd heard the judge on television saying he'd be here. . . .

"Look," he said, "why don't you get on with the interrogation, rather than asking me all these pointless questions about how long I've had the ticket. . . ."

That's part of the method, but he's not to know that. Get him stirred up inside. Get him angry, puzzled, upset. Make him ask himself why, and what . . .

"If that's the way you want it. . . . I think you planted a bomb here tonight. In a microphone. With the intention of killing the judge. I've moved that microphone out of the Hall . . ." Watch his face, watch his eyes, the corners of his mouth—no, he shows nothing—"But you may have planted another, in case the first one didn't go off. I can understand why you hate the judge . . ."

"But I don't. That's where you're wrong. I don't hate anybody."

"Then why did you threaten him in court?"

"Hot air, hot air. They were expecting a scene from me

in court and I gave 'em one. I gave 'em one all right." Dammit, he chuckled. "It made every newspaper in the country. . . ."

Keep him confident. Keep him going. But make it quick.

"In the old days, where did you learn to make bombs?"

"It may surprise you to know I'm a Bachelor of Science. . ."

"Bachelor of Science, eh?"—as if I didn't believe him.

"Yes, chemistry. It's true."

I hoped my face said "Pull the other one, it's got bells on it!"

"We could check that . . ."

"Why don't you? I've still got my degree certificate."

Now he was truculent, and defiance comes next. Anyway, he's lost that cheekiness that was like an impenetrable wall. This is the danger point in any interview. Now he could go either of two ways. If he's defiant he'll either want to boast about his achievements and tell me everything I want to know just to prove he's a better man than I am, or he'll clam up and defy me to beat it out of him. And that would mean a long slow interrogation, with three of us firing questions at him day and night, refusing to let him rest until he's told us what we want to know, pestering him, confusing him, dragging it out of him by sheer persistence.

"Oh God," I thought, "don't let this be like that. There isn't all that much time left. Make him want to tell me what I want to know. Let him be defiant, let him prove he's a better man than I am. I don't mind how many points he scores off me, just so long as he tells me where the bomb is. If there's a bomb. Thousands of people out there depend on me. Don't let this be another goof."

"Is there a bomb in the Hall, Harrigan, yes or no?"

He didn't speak.

Right. This is it. The final gamble. The last chip that either scoops the pot, or loses all. For the last time, I hit him.

It was a bone-cracking smash with the back of my hand that rocked him on his seat, sprang tears into his eyes. He hadn't been expecting it and the shock really hurt him, and then when I raised my other hand he held out his hand towards me. He'd had enough. I'd had enough. "Is there a bomb in the Hall, Harrigan?"

"They cured me of bombs in the prison hospital. The psychiatrist . . . cured me . . . of bombs . . ." His speech was blurred, indistinct. I'd damaged his plate, probably cut his tongue, perhaps even dislocated his jaw. He fainted, and flopped off the chair like an india-rubber man. I turned him over onto his back, opened his collar, loosened his tie. There was nothing else I could do for him. Nothing else anyone could do for him, except give him time to recover.

Flughafer was on the repeat of the first choral stanza. "All mankind are brothers plighted, where thy gentle wings abide."

No bomb. That's what Harrigan said. I believed him. First feeling a sense of utter relief. No bomb. No explosion. No carnage, no rubble and digging out the pieces of humans, no listening to the cries of men and women and children trapped beneath rubble while the bulldozers clear a path towards them and then, at the last, we inch our way forward, a brick at a time. I've pulled the remains of men out of car smashes, a train accident once, and I can't stand any more of that. No one can describe what it feels to find a recognisable human limb still clad in the tattered remnants of a pair of trousers, a sock, a shoe. Thank God, no bomb.

But the second feeling, edging out that first sense of relief, was the knowledge of my own foolishness. I'd put the entire division at panic stations because I'd thought I recognised Harrigan's face in the crowd. I'd disrupted the lives of countless people, caused people to be pulled out of their homes, all because I'd seen Harrigan in the Hall. But, what was more unforgivable, I'd beaten a man unmercifully, and I would never forget that. My conscience was quite clear, but I knew I'd taken a gamble and lost.

The law would take its inevitable course. I'd be suspended, prosecuted, dismissed from the force, gaoled. A copper gone wrong can expect no leniency. And I'd gone terribly, brutally, indefensibly wrong, and a judge had been there long enough to confirm it. Harrigan would be compensated financially, but once a man has been beaten like that he can never face life with the same confidence again.

What the hell; the police force was the wrong place for me anyway. How many times had I gone wrong in the past. I'd had brilliant successes. I'd nobbled the Keiller gang, George West, the multiple murderer, the Jackson brothers, Billy the Axeman. A drawer full of commendations. But how many Maurice Brighams had there been? And if it came to that, how many Susans? Where was Susan now? In a bathroom with her wrists slashed, in the ladies' toilet of a railway station full of sleeping pills? Or in bed with some laughing lad? All because my vanity wouldn't let her find her own level in life.

Now, at long last, I could understand the chief's attitude towards me over the years. I'd been his protégé, but by God I must have been a pain in the arse to him, the brilliant pupil who never quite makes it. And they'd nail me, and put me inside, and I'd serve a year for assault. Some good would come of it for me. I'd be young enough to make a different life for myself, for Sarah and the kids, when I came out. Sarah would stick by me, and I'd find myself a real job of work. I was a good driver, a good admin man. I might even make a good salesman. But I wouldn't be a copper.

I went to the door and opened it. "Come in here, Skelton."

He came in, looked at me with an unspoken list of questions long as a report form. He looked at Harrigan, knew I'd thumped him, and wanted no part of it. Nothing personal. No criticism. Just self-protection. He stood by the door, his hand on the knob. Harrigan was still unconscious. For all Skelton knew, he could be dead.

"Shall I get Cooper?" he asked, meaning, "Begging your pardon, Inspector, but I want Cooper in here as a witness. I had no part in what's been done to the suspect."

He opened the door again and called down the corridor, but already Cooper was standing by the doorway. He came in, looked at Harrigan, and smiled. What gets into such a man? He looked at Skelton, but not at me. He looked at his watch. "At such and such time on such and such a day, I was called in . . ." I left them together to confirm alibis and do what they could for Harrigan. They weren't brutes; they'd help him. The judge and Sergeant Bates were looking into the auditorium, listening to the music. Sergeant Bates was bored but trying to hide it; although the judge was fascinated by the performance, he saw me approach. When I beckoned he came towards me. Sergeant Bates stayed where he was. The judge, tall and thin, walked towards me like a lion stalking his prey. I turned and he followed me to the outside of Barrett's office. The door was closed. He stood waiting, a patient man who knew his time could come.

"Harrigan says there was no bomb."

"And you believe him."

I nodded my head. His eyes bored into my inner being.

"You've struck that man, haven't you?"

"Yes, sir."

"That's deplorable . . ."

"I know it is, sir, and so is planting a bomb in a girls' school."

"Don't bandy words with me. What the devil is this

country coming to if we cannot even rely on the officers of the law not to behave like animals."

"Unless I could quickly satisfy myself no bomb was in that Hall I was going to have to take the risk of clearing the people out. I didn't know where the bomb might be, what sort of fuse and detonator it might have. It was quite conceivable that *any* disturbance in that Hall could have set the bomb working, and I needn't tell you what that would have meant in a crowd of over four thousand people."

"I presume you are rehearsing the statement you will make when you are charged with assault, Inspector."

He went into the room. Skelton and Cooper came out. Skelton cocked an eyebrow at me and said nothing. Cooper appeared to be smirking but that may have been my imagination, fed by my intense dislike of him. I waited in the corridor looking at my watch. The Choral Symphony would soon be over. Soon we'd know if the anonymous note, as everyone had said, was a student prank or not. After two minutes the judge opened the door, and I went in.

"I cannot recall a single occasion on which I was more distressed than I am now," he said. "How any officer of the police force can treat a human being as you have treated this one is totally beyond my comprehension. Your two men tell me you were alone with this man, and remained alone with him for quite some time. They have assured me that you, and you alone, are responsible for the condition in which I find this man. I'm not vengeful, Inspector, believe me, but the knowledge that the law will doubtless deal with you as you deserve is a source of personal satisfaction to me. I am going back to my box to collect my hat and my coat, and then I shall want to see your superintendent. I have left instructions with your two men outside that, until senior officer sees Mr. Harrigan, you are not to be left alone with him."

That was his final word. He walked across the office, flung open the door, and waited for me to precede him. Both Skelton and Cooper avoided my eye.

We walked down the corridor in a tumult of sound from the orchestra and the full chorus and soloists.

> WORLD DOST FEEL THY MAKER NEAR
> SEEK HIM O'ER YON STARRY SPHERE
> SURE THERE LIVES A LOVING FATHER . . .

We turned the corner and the judge went towards his box. I stood watching the four soloists on each side and to the front of Otto Flughafer, singing with all their hearts and voices the last words of Schiller's *Ode to Joy*. "Father lives, Father, Father lives . . ." and then the orchestra ran alone into the last few bars of music.

The applause began as the choir and soloists ended, laced under the last bars from the orchestra, and swelled to flood-tide when the last notes were cut off by that imperious wave of Flughafer's hand. No stunned silence, none of that often phoney hush that follows an indifferent performance. What little I'd been able to listen to had convinced me this was a truly great performance. The audience loved it and nothing would prevent them showing it. Flughafer turned to face the audience and stood quite still for a moment, knowing his reputation was formed. He turned and beckoned for the musicians to stand and the soloists to come forward, but they all disobeyed him. Faugeras, smiling, remained seated. This moment belonged to Flughafer, this praise was Flughafer's salute, and the orchestra and choir clapped with the audience. Flughafer turned back and bowed deeply, gratefully, a huge smile of overwhelming joy on his face. Even from that distance I could see his eyes were raining tears. He stood erect, proud, quite overcome by the emotion of his triumph that no one could deny him, the superb triumph of a public acclamation of his genius.

And then he started to fall, and fell slowly forward, down, flat on his face, and I knew he was dead before he hit the edge of the platform and went over it like a rag doll.

I ran down the aisle pushing people aside. Sergeant Bates ran with me. The applause continued from the back of the Hall since, with so many standing at the front, few could see what had happened to Flughafer.

A man came out of the third row of the centre block and he too ran forward, thrusting people aside in his attempt to get through. He was carrying a black bag. A *black bag.* I bounced and cannoned off people stepping out into the aisle and heard them protest but Sergeant Bates and I continued forward in that flying wedge and I dived long and low at the running man as he reached the bottom of the aisle and brought him skidding down from behind and he slid forward and his head banged against the woodwork of the platform and I held on to his ankle.

Now the audience was shouting and screams and pandemonium had broken out behind us and above in the circle where they could all see everything that was happening, but I left the man to Sergeant Bates and picked myself up and fought through the knot of people who'd surged forward to look at Flughafer. And now my elbow went in and my shoulder. "Get back, Police," I shouted, plucking them aside. "Get back, get back, damn you," and they slowly obeyed me and cleared a path so that I could reach Flughafer, a pool of silence amidst the excited cacophony that filled the Hall.

He was dead.

How had it been done? A knife? A dart? I'd heard no sound of a gun but with a silencer I couldn't have heard it above the applause. Damn Harrigan and the judge, damn them, damn them. First rule of a copper's life is not to be hypnotised by the obvious. Look for the wood among the trees. Don't let yourself get so involved in one part of an investigation so deeply you miss the other possibilities.

My tackle had momentarily winded the running man and he was gasping for breath. His hand still clutched a well-worn black bag and the sergeant had forced him through the crowd to my side. Quickly I ran my hands over him, then snatched the bag from him. Maybe he'd dumped whatever he'd used, the blowpipe, the pistol, the bow, under the seat, hoping to make his escape in the general confusion. He hadn't counted on policemen being in the Hall. By now he'd thought to be a half a mile down the road.

"Get on that platform," I said to Bates, "and bang that drum so's everybody will listen, and get 'em all sitting in their seats."

The running man had recovered enough of his breath to speak.

"Let me go to him," he said, "I'm his doctor . . ."

"You're his *what?*" His words were like a cold douche in my face. I had a premonition of impending disaster.

"I'm Otto Flughafer's doctor, you cretin," he said.

I let him go. By now Bates had instructed the timpanist who was banging the big drum urgently while the sergeant shouted for everybody to sit down again.

Together we went to Flughafer, the doctor and I. He opened the well-worn black bag in which I'd thought to find an assassin's weapon, but from it he produced a stethoscope. He did the things a doctor does, pulse, heart beat, eyelids, but didn't need his qualifications to tell him Flughafer was dead. I've seen 'em. Lots of 'em. If you have too fertile an imagination you suspect cyanide poisoning; the victim's limbs are often twisted, his mouth and lips often tinged with blue. But there's no smell of bitter almonds.

You know the heart has stopped.

From the back of the Hall I heard the separate voices of the superintendent and the chief inspector, shouting for everyone to sit down. The people were going back to their seats, sitting down. An awful calm descended on the Hall and all I could hear was an inner voice saying "This time, Inspector Armstrong, you've really done it. . . ."

"A heart attack, Doctor?"

"Sort of . . ."

Faugeras walked across towards us. *"Il est mort?"*

The doctor looked up at him. *"Oui, il est mort."*

I could see tears start to form in Faugeras's eyes, and then he walked back to his seat and sat down, his face stony.

"What was it?" I asked the doctor.

"You're a policeman, I take it?"

"Yes, a detective inspector."

"I see. Well, he died of an embolism."

He produced a card from his top pocket and handed it to me. Gordon Frior, M.D., with an address in Eaton Square. I looked at the card, looked at him, looked down at Flughafer's corpse.

"He wasn't strong enough to conduct, but he insisted. It was his start. He was a brilliant student, but he had a cerebral aneurism."

"And you're willing to certify that as the cause of death?"

He looked at me for hidden meanings. I had none. I was clutching at straws. A drowning man. The chief inspector and the superintendent were marching down the aisle towards me, slowly, as befitted their dignity and the gravity of the occasion, but purposefully, like two undertakers.

"There'll be a post-mortem, of course, but I'd write a certificate immediately. He was my patient; I saw him every few days for the past month or more; I've had him in St. George's Hospital for observation and investigation.

There's no doubt in my mind. He had a cerebral aneurism. Under the strain of conducting, that aneurism burst. I knew it would. I told him not to conduct this evening. But he insisted. A doctor's powers only extend so far, you know, Inspector." He was talking too much. He knew it; I knew it; and the corpse of Otto Flughafer lay between us.

"This gentleman is the doctor of the deceased, Chief Inspector," I said. "He's certain that death was caused by a cerebral aneurism."

"You'll want a post-mortem of course," the superintendent said.

"Of course."

"Pathologist?"

"Is that necessary?"

"I think the superintendent would prefer him to come here," the chief inspector said. "It won't take long."

"Get some screens from somewhere," I said to Sergeant Bates.

The doctor was agitated; not because his professional integrity was being questioned, I suspected, but out of compassion for the patient lying at our feet in sight of over four thousand people. He took off his top coat, and placed it over Otto Flughafer's face. "Can't we get an ambulance, and take him out of here?" he asked.

It was my case. I hadn't been taken off it just because the chief inspector and the chief superintendent were there. "Can you definitely certify the cause of death?" I asked the doctor.

"I've already told you, yes."

"Can you certify that Flughafer didn't die as a result of a wound?"

"A wound?"

"A wound."

"With what?"

"With a dart, a knife, an arrow, the bullet from a silenced gun . . ."

"Are you out of your mind?" he asked. He turned to the chief superintendent. "Look, what's all this about? Mr. Flughafer died of an aneurism. Nothing else. I can see it by looking at him. I know from my professional knowledge and training that the post-mortem examination will merely confirm what I can see with my own two eyes. Isn't that good enough for you?"

"With your permission, Chief Superintendent," I said, "I'd like to clear the Hall. But I'd like a pathologist to come here to examine Mr. Flughafer before he is moved, and I'd like to ask the judge if he would be so good as to stay. I also intend to hang on to Harrigan."

He nodded his head. James Barrett had been hovering at the side of the platform. I beckoned for him to come over to me. He did so. Meanwhile I instructed one of the constables, "Find the judge in Box 22F, and ask him if he'd be good enough to wait in his box until I come to see him. Meanwhile, we're going to clear the Hall. I want a man on every exit, just checking, looking for any irregularities. I don't anticipate they'll find anything, but I just want to check. Anybody with form, any of our old customers, hold 'em 'til the crowd's gone, okay?"

He set off in the direction of the judge's box.

When James Barrett arrived I introduced him to the chief superintendent and the chief inspector. Neither said anything, neither shook hands.

"This is Mr. Flughafer's doctor," I said, "and he assured us that Mr. Flughafer died of a cerebral aneurism . . ."

"What's that?" Barrett asked.

"A blood vessel that burst, in his brain," I said, looking at the doctor for confirmation of my layman's diagnosis. He nodded. "Now, Mr. Barrett, can you clear the Hall for us?

As quickly and as quietly as possible? What will you do? Abandon the concert? Give 'em their money back?"

"That'll hardly be necessary . . ." he said.

He walked into the centre of the platform, cleared his throat. The Hall was as silent as if he'd been about to start a symphony.

"My name is James Barrett," he said, "and I am the manager. It is my painful and sorrowful duty to tell you that Mr. Flughafer has passed away. In the circumstances I know you will agree that the rest of the concert should be cancelled. We'd be most grateful if you could all leave the Hall, as quietly as possible. Could we start here at the front and show our respect by filing out, row by row?" He glanced at the men sitting on the aisles in the front row. The men got up and started to walk down the aisle. Slowly, the rest of the row followed them, then the second row, then the third. I could see the judge still sitting in his box, obviously waiting as I had asked. Sergeant Bates had put the screens around Flughafer, and the doctor and the chief superintendent were in there with the chief inspector, no doubt going through the symptoms of aneurisms as an academic exercise. Pierre Faugeras wiped his eyes, stood up, and with his violin held in his hand he led the way off the platform. The orchestra, the soloists, and then the choir all followed him slowly, nobody speaking.

I sat in the seat at the end of the first row. The chief superintendent came from behind the screen and walked to the side of the platform, to go out through that door. He never even glanced at me. The chief inspector came out. "I'll pop outside for a minute, lad, and then I'll be back." He was going to call off the dogs, to send the Army home, the ambulances, all except the one they'd use to take the body of Flughafer to the mortuary, to get the coppers back on their beats and the people back into their houses from which I had caused them to be evacuated. The doctor came from behind the screen, and sat beside me. "You never told me how the police got here so quickly," he said. I guessed he'd asked the chief superintendent and got a flea in his ear.

Suddenly I thought I could understand everything. My brain was no longer tired, no longer preoccupied with my own fate. Hippocratic oath, that's what they call it. No doctor is allowed to betray the confidences of a patient. Wasn't there a fuss when Winston Churchill's doctor spoke about his patient even after Churchill died? A young man comes to see you in your Eaton Square practice. No doubt he's sent by an old friend and patient, a professor of music at the Royal College. It's a certain fact that Flughafer, a young student just starting to make his way, couldn't have afforded Gordon Frior. Perhaps the professor rings you—"I'm sending one of my students to you. See if you can fix him up. He's a brilliant chap with a great future so see what you can do." But you discover this brilliant young chap has no future at all. A cerebral aneurism. The dilation of a blood vessel in the brain. It's like a small balloon, blown in the actual tissue of the walls of the blood vessel, standing out in the brain weak and throbbing and likely to burst at any moment. How do I know? I arrested a man with one. I pushed him into a car. He fell in, dead. They accused me of police brutality, said I'd thumped him. An aneurism can burst at any time. What could Dr. Frior do? Get the boy to hospital?

Aneurisms are tricky things to deal with. You can tie them off back and front and drain the blood from them. If you can get at them. A lot of them are difficult to get at. In the brain this one would be a bastard. They'd have the boy on the operating table for hours with his head open, trying to find the aneurism among the blood and tissue and bone. One slip of the scalpel a hundredth of an inch one way or the other and the boy would never waken again. And while the surgeon was probing about, looking, feeling, testing, the anaesthetist would be studying his machine, studying the patient's reactions, and his ability to resist the shocks. When the patient had had enough, the anaesthetist and the the cardiac specialist would say "no more, no more" and the surgeon would sew the boy's head and leave the operating theatre a disappointed man. The boy would come to, eventually, escaping from those anaesthetic nightmares that probably sent musical notes shaped like devils scudding across a field of sharpened staves, and Dr. Frior would go into the hospital to lie to him. "You're all right now," he'd say. "The operation wasn't a total success, but you're all right." Only when the boy had recovered his strength would the doctor break to him the narrow difference between "not a total success" and "complete failure." "But am I all right?" the boy would ask, already sitting up in bed and reading music scores the way other patients read thrillers and sex books. The boy would expect to be out again soon. You'd told him he wouldn't be in for a long time, and already he'd be counting the days. And when he saw your unsmiling face, he'd insist you told him the truth. What was the truth? He'd given up a term of music to prepare for the operation. When he came round and the scars of the probing knives were still fresh on his brain, you'd have to tell him that his head had been opened for nothing. Who'd be a doctor?

"Greatness is a mysterious quality, Inspector," Dr. Frior was saying to me. "Who knows what makes it? Who knows where the tissue of the brain can take us? The sheer tissue. Mozart was a musical genius because of the workings of the tissues of his brain. Degas, da Vinci, Winston Churchill, Einstein, all geniuses because that inconsequential grey matter was arranged in a certain incomprehensible way. And we were proposing to cut into this tissue, possibly to destroy those very cells which might have accounted for this boy's remarkable musical ability. If he'd lived he could easily have been another Beecham, Sargent, Bolt, Bernstein. Everyone who knew him was convinced he was destined for the top of the musical tree. When I told him the operation had been a failure, he closed back in on himself like a snail. His actual operation healed quickly and he went back to music school to cram twenty hours of living into each day, eight days into each brief week. Living a world of music. He came to see me every week, sometimes twice a week. Headaches, mostly. I prescribed a palliative for him, a pain-killer, but all the time each of us knew that damned balloon, that aneurism, was throbbing away inside his head, and could burst at any moment.

"And then, he received this invitation to conduct the Beethoven. They only asked him because the Russian had to withdraw and all the top-line conductors were booked. I warned him. 'Conduct that concert,' I said to him, 'and you'll be dead.' The sheer physical energy required was bound to kill him. I can remember him now sitting in my drawing-room. I'd got to know him too well for him to come to the surgery. I argued with him, pleaded with him, tried every way I knew how to get him not to conduct."

"You could do nothing for him, medically?" I asked.

He thought for a moment. "That was the worst part of it," he said. "Yes, there was something that could be done. A very simple operation. Tie the rising artery at the neck, just up here." He indicated a spot on his own neck just behind his ear.

"And that would have cured him?"

"It would have prevented the aneurism ever growing, and if it couldn't grow, it wouldn't burst."

"In God's name why didn't you do it?"

"It's a successful operation. It stops the aneurism. But it has a side effect. In fifty per cent of the cases, the patient becomes paralysed down one side."

Paralysed down one side. No music, since all instruments require both hands, or at least the ability to coordinate the movements of your fingers. And who's ever heard of a one-armed conductor? "He wouldn't agree to the operation?"

"He wouldn't even consider it. You could hardly blame him. 'You've had my head open once,' he said, 'with no result. Now you want to open my neck and you say there's a fifty-fifty chance I'll be paralysed when you've finished. Nothing doing, Doctor, nothing doing."

"And so you let him walk on that platform tonight, knowing that most probably he wouldn't walk off it?" I stood up, but not to stretch my legs. I wanted to look at a man who could do a thing like that, look him full in the face.

"It wasn't a certainty . . ."

"All right, what are the odds, Dr. Frior? What odds would you give him on ending the concert alive? Fifty to one against? A hundred to one?"

"Even if it were a thousand to one against, he still had a chance."

And then I saw it. "You tried to reason with him?"

"Yes."

"Tried to persuade him not to conduct?"

"Yes, yes."

"And when that failed, remembering you could say nothing to anyone without contravening your precious doctor-patient oath, you decided to do the next best thing and send the manager an anonymous note. . . . *You* wanted the concert stopped. To save Flughafer's life. And you couldn't think of any other way of doing it."

He jumped from his seat, his eyes blazing. "What are you saying? I sent an *anonymous note?* Here? To stop the concert? I did no such thing. Has a note been received?"

"You didn't know?" My disbelief must have shown in my voice for he seized me by the lapels of my jacket. "It's inconceivable that I should do such a thing. An anonymous note? To save the life of my own patient. It's out of the question, do you hear, out of the question. . . ."

As gently as possible I pulled my lapels from his grasp. It was my only decent suit.

"Why didn't you notify the police . . . ?"

"I couldn't, Inspector. If other people's lives had been involved, if he'd been an airline pilot about to take a flight, that would have been different. I would have been quite justified in notifying the appropriate authorities to have him grounded, if he wouldn't listen to me. But this was different. No one else was involved."

He glared at me, still angry. But I wasn't moved. I kept telling myself this was the man who'd permitted Otto Flughafer to stand on that platform and kill himself in front of four thousand people, who'd sat there and watched while a brilliant young man destroyed himself. Something of what I was thinking must have crossed my face, some fleeting contempt.

"It's hard for you to understand, isn't it?" he asked. "It's not something you can write books of rules about. It has to do with a man and his doctor, with the nature of medicine itself. Without this feeling no doctor could carry on the practice of medicine, and no patient would ever trust him. Do you realise that?"

"This man killed himself and you let him. If we catch a man trying to kill himself we lock him up to prevent it. In ninety-nine cases out of a hundred, he forgets all about it by the next day, and we can let him go home with an easy conscience. Sometimes the man is so sick, we turn him over to a doctor, and like as not the doctor cures him. But if we can't persuade the man, and the doctor can't help him, we have the man certified of unsound mind, and put away for his own good. To keep him alive, and out of mischief."

Dr. Frior shook his head, but not to argue with me. We

couldn't argue since there was no common ground. This man had been compelled by his beliefs to sit for seventy-one minutes and watch a man killing himself. At any time he could have shouted "Stop the concert." Flughafer would have been mad at him, but a doctor is not in practice to stay popular. I accept there are times a doctor must turn away and give up the struggle, letting his patient quietly slip away into death. But Flughafer had a useful lifetime in front of him, though with limitations he could surely have been persuaded to accept. And this man let him kill himself.

"You say you received an anonymous note?" Frior repeated.

"Not me. The manager. Just before the concert started. He didn't take it seriously in view of the student demo."

"What did the note say? Are you allowed to tell me?"

"Certainly. It said, 'AT THE END OF THE CHORAL SYMPHONY, YOU'LL HAVE A DEATH ON YOUR HANDS.' "

"Curious wording. Don't they usually threaten? It sounds as if this was meant to 'inform' not threaten. As if someone was saying, "Sorry for the bother, but I'm afraid that after the Choral Symphony you'll have all the inconvenience of a death on your hands." On your hands. As if whoever wrote the note was saying, 'best be prepared,' 'best have an ambulance ready and waiting.' See what I mean?"

Yes, I *did* see what he meant. "What sort of a chap was Otto Flughafer? Personally?"

"Very shy, very diffident, except in musical matters. He hated anyone going to any trouble on his behalf . . ."

"He didn't like to 'inconvenience' people . . . ?"

"That's right. He hated to be—as he put it—a 'bother to anyone.' "

We were both silent. It was inconceivable, fantastic, but in character. I'm sorry, but I'm going to conduct the Choral

Symphony and they tell me I will die. It will be a bit of "a bother" to you, to have "a death on your hands."

Unbelievable that anyone could be so considerate of others.

"He sent the note himself," Dr. Frior said.

Was it possible? That Otto Flughafer wanted to be named as the conductor of the Paris State Orchestra. He wanted to rehearse them, mould them to produce his interpretation of the Beethoven symphony. No one could take that away from him. Before he died, he would hear his own conception of that classic work, performed by a professional orchestra. Of course, even rehearsing the orchestra he ran a risk his embolism would burst. Sometime, in that vast night stillness when all such thoughts are born, he'd told himself, "If I can't conduct the Paris State Orchestra and create that Beethoven symphony, I don't want to live." Many people say things like that. Few have the strength to mean them. Susan had said it on the telephone. That was what she had said. "I've let you down, I want to die." Flughafer said, "Without the Beethoven, I want to die." Same thing, merely a difference in calibre. For Flughafer, a life without his type of music was inconceivable. For Susan, a life without my continuing approval was, even if only momentarily, inconceivable. Flughafer had the strength of will and purpose to continue down that road of no return, even to the extent of conducting the work standing up in public, with all its consequent physical strain, and the near certainty of death. Did Susan have the will and purpose to carry out her intention? Or was her threat no more than the idle remark of an immature person?

I had no knowledge to help me. I had never wanted anything badly enough to be prepared to die for it. One could argue that every day I risk dying on the police force, every day I deliberately expose myself to a different death. But

I'd never consciously said, "I want that and if I can't have it, I'd rather die."

"Many people try to commit suicide," Dr. Frior was saying, "and fortunately many of those who try don't succeed. They change their minds at the last moment. Unfortunately, for many of them, that 'last moment' is already too late."

It must be the ultimate irony to die when you've changed your mind, when you've found some reason, however slender, for staying alive. "You really think he sent the note, Doctor?"

"Yes, I do. . . ."

Otto Flughafer had meant it not as a warning, but as a kindness. He might not have realised the manager always went into his office as soon as a concert had started. It would be logical to assume the manager would stay out in the Hall, at least until well into the first piece to be played. In which case, the note wouldn't have been found so soon, we wouldn't have got there so soon. But at least we'd have been alerted, and possibly an ambulance might have already been standing by. Flughafer might not have wanted the Ninth Symphony stopped, just someone "standing by" in case he died. He could slip the note onto the manager's desk while the audience was arriving, knowing Barrett would be too busy to go in there until the audience was seated, and the concert about to begin.

"He hoped the manager would come on stage and stop the concert," Frior said.

"To make Otto Flughafer the innocent victim of circumstances but, nevertheless, a man who'd conducted the Paris State Symphony Orchestra!" Part of me wanted to believe he'd not changed his mind, even at the last moment. Part of me wanted to believe he'd made the decision to conduct and die, and had stuck by it from the beginning. But death is a shocking waste, especially the death of a boy of such promise as Flughafer.

The last of the audience was leaving. We got up. I started to walk along the aisle towards the manager's office. Now I had to face Harrigan again, and the consequences of my actions. He'd sue me for assault, of course. The judge would see to that. It'd make all the papers, no doubt. I was going to ask the doctor, Frior, to take a look at him, but decided against it. They'd suspect I was trying to get off the hook. No, when the pathologist, who'd be here in a minute, had looked at what was left of Flughafer, he could look at Harrigan. There'd be a scene-of-the-crime team with a photographer, and the superintendent would want a record of the way I'd left Harrigan, blood and bruises and all.

But there was one thing I had to do before anybody got to him.

Harrigan was sitting in the chair where I had left him. His face was a shocking mess. Cooper one side of him, Skelton the other, and they assisted him out of the manager's office, and along the corridor, to the judge's box. When the judge saw Harrigan he leaped from the chair on which he had been sitting and they let Harrigan sit there. He was conscious, but only just, and the side of one eye had swollen so badly he could hardly see out of it.

The judge was looking at me. "What causes animals like you?" he said, his voice quiet but full of a deep disgust.

"They'll be here soon," I said, "and I shall ask the police pathologist to look at him . . ."

"It's a bed in hospital he wants, man, not a police pathologist."

"If that's what he needs, sir, I'll get him one as quickly as I can."

"Then why have you brought him in here to me?"

I beckoned for Cooper and Skelton to leave us, just the three of us together. From where I was standing in the box

I could see the pathologist arrive and with him the incidents team. Dr. Frior was talking to the pathologist, doubtless giving Flughafer's medical history. But none of that concerned me. I was off the case; I was off the force; the chief superintendent would officially suspend me the next time he saw me.

"An anonymous note had been received, Judge. I began to investigate it. I located Harrigan in the Hall and discovered he had a record as a mad bomber. Furthermore, I learned that he'd threatened to kill you when you sentenced him, and then I discovered you were in the Hall."

"Look here, man," he said, "I will not be involved in this any more than I have already been. So far as I am concerned you have been guilty of a grievous assault on this man. If you've brought him to me hoping I will intercede on your behalf, I'm afraid you are wasting your time, and his. What you have done to this man is quite inexcusable on the strength of a personal suspicion, a whim; if you had had evidence, there might just possibly have been grounds for it, though I doubt even that. The best thing you can do is get out of my sight. Leave that man here; I'll attend to him and see that he gets whatever attention he needs."

Harrigan was beginning to revive, and turned his head at the sound of our voices, though he had not yet properly recovered consciousness.

"I'll ask the pathologist to come here as soon as he has finished with Mr. Flughafer," I said. "The chief superintendent will want an official examination made." I left the box. All right, it was true. I had wanted the judge to intercede on my behalf. It was a gamble. I thought that seeing Harrigan he would realise I couldn't beat a man like that unless I was *convinced* I had good reasons for so doing. I had hoped, just for a moment, the judge would accept that I had been doing what I considered to be my duty, no matter how difficult or unpleasant, how vicious, it had turned out to be. But judges are trained to examine evidence; their gods are "proved" and "not proved," "relevant" or "irrelevant." My suspicions had been "not proved" and "irrelevant"; I'd lost on both counts.

On the way into the Hall I met the Army officer from Bomb Disposal. "Nothing in that microphone, Inspector."

I nodded.

He thrust a pad at me. "Care to sign the chitty?" It was titled "Incident Report." I scrawled my name across the bottom and left him to fill in the details.

"Don't worry, Inspector," he said. "It happens to us all the time."

Barrett was next in line. "I've spoken to the chairman," he said. "I've given him a full account. He was very angry. He said I ought to have spoken to him earlier, that he would have authorised me to stop the concert. And then that poor boy might not have died. As it is, you'll have that on your conscience for the rest of your life."

There should have been an answer, a short one line get to hell. But I couldn't find it, and even if I had, I doubt I would have used it on Barrett. This Hall was his life, his world, his womb. I didn't speak, watched him mince across the carpet, a quivering mass of resentment and anger. I looked around the Hall empty of audience, silent of sound. The commissionaires, the electricians, the sweepers and cleaners, Barrett, even we, the police, didn't count. We were the functionaries who served the Hall's purpose; orchestras and audiences were its reason. Sarah and I, we should start going to concerts again. And we should bring the kids.

A young girl approached me. "Inspector Armstrong?"

"Yes."

"Sorry I'm late. I thought they said the *Albert* Hall. I'm from the BBC. I was told you wanted me to show you the control panel in the box. . . ."

I'd forgotten all about the BBC, and the studio manager on the other end of the line. "Go into the box," I said, "and tell that young man it's all over and I'll be in touch with him."

"You wouldn't like to sign my expenses voucher," she said, "so that I can claim for the taxi?"

I scribbled my name on the piece of paper she held towards me.

Cooper was carrying Harrigan's bag. Taking it to the judge's box, seeking another chance to put in the knife. "Have you checked everything's in there?" I asked him. He opened the bag and produced a list of contents. I made him check each item. When he came to the last, a transistor radio, he said, "Better make sure it still works," and switched it on. No music came from it, so I told him to switch it off and put it back inside the bag.

I walked away from him but I'd gone only two paces when a fanlight across the Hall shattered from outside when it was hit by the first bullet from the magazine of the Bren gun, which looked like a microphone mounted on the roof and was radio-operated. Cooper had activated the firing mechanism. One by one the other bullets from the magazine whanged across the Hall in rapid fire and sprayed their target, the inside of Box 22F. By then I was running madly along the corridor. When the magazine emptied itself, the firing stopped and I went into the judge's box. Harrigan, sitting in the judge's chair, had taken most of the bullets in his chest. Or what was left of his chest. The judge was standing at the side of the box, half into his raincoat. A trickle of blood ran down his arm where a bullet had got him.

"At this moment, your honour," I said to the judge, "four thousand people could have been trying to get out of this Hall." I turned round and left the box, my insides churning. I walked along the corridor. I could hear shouts and pounding feet as the chief inspector, the chief superintendent, and their band of men came rushing into the Hall.

The telephone was ringing along the corridor. I picked it up. It was Arthur.

"Lucky you rang me when you did," he said. "We found her. In a bathroom. At the hostel. My constable broke down the door. She was in the bath. She'd opened both her wrists. But we got there in time."

I hung up the telephone, then dialled Sarah's number to tell her I'd be late.

They found a thumbprint on one of the bullet cases. Mad Mike Harrigan's, of course.

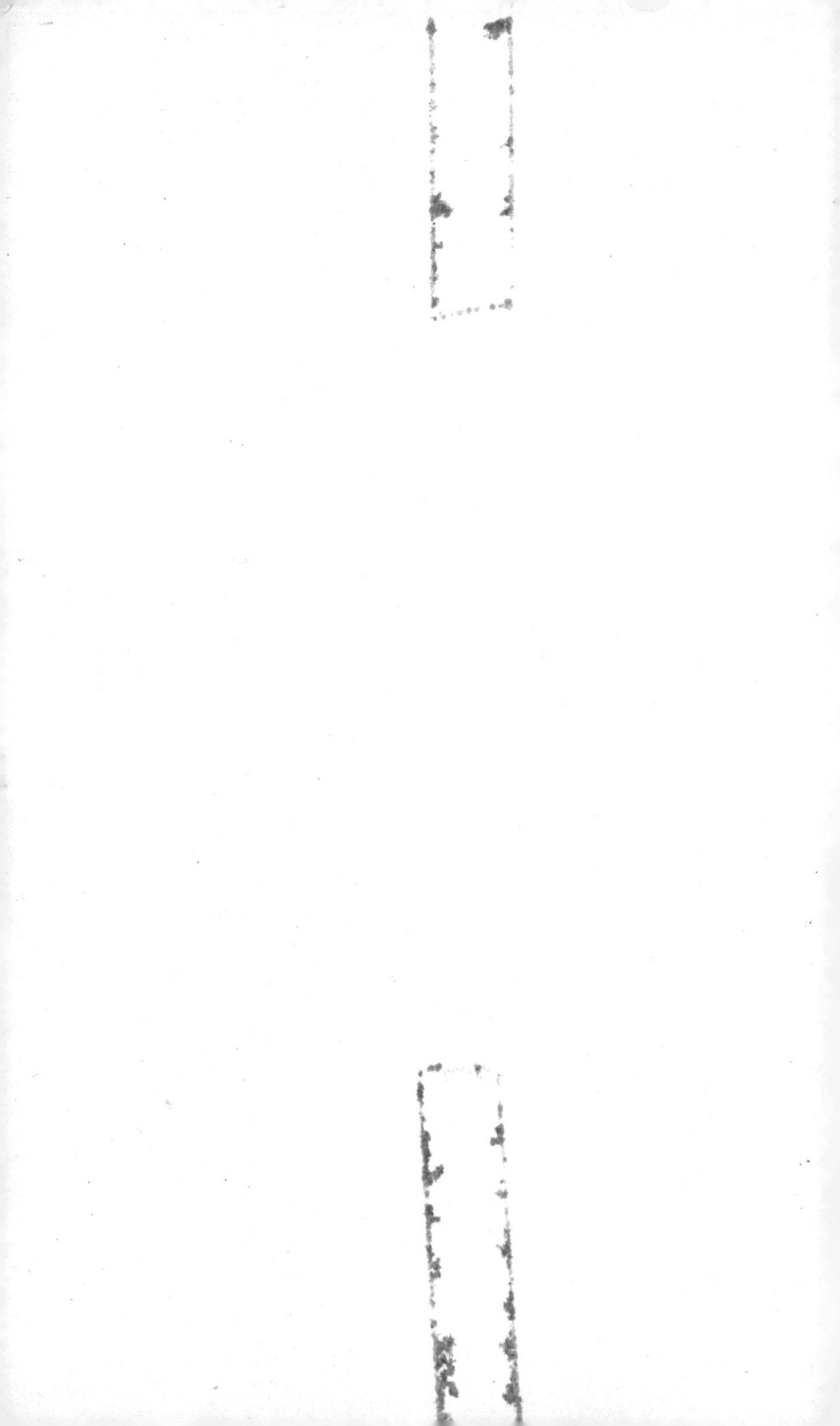